# CASTLE ROCK

***Other Five Star Titles
by Carolyn G. Hart:***

Brave Hearts
Crime on Her Mind
The Devereaux Legacy
Flee from the Past

# CASTLE ROCK

## Carolyn G. Hart

**Five Star**
**Unity, Maine**

Five Star Mystery
Published in conjunction with Tekno Books and Ed Gorman.

Cover photograph © Alan J. La Vallee

March 2000

Five Star Standard Print Mystery Series.

The text of this edition is unabridged.

Set in 11 pt. Plantin by Rick Gundberg.

Printed in the United States on permanent paper.

**Library of Congress Cataloging-in-Publication Data**

Hart, Carolyn G.
   Castle rock / Carolyn G. Hart.
     p.  cm.
   ISBN 0-7862-2365-0 (hc : alk. paper)
   1. Ranch life — Fiction. I. Title.
 PS3558.A676 C37  2000
  813′.54—dc21                      99-059541

# CASTLE ROCK

CASTLE ROCK

# One

It was dangerous. Serena knew that, but she had always been a fool for danger. She bent a little closer to Hurricane's neck and urged him to go even faster. Behind her, above the clatter of the horses' hooves and the rattle of stones falling from the narrow trail, she heard Jed's shout.

"Serena, stop! For God's sake, you little fool, stop!"

A tiny smile flickered on her intent face, but, eyes narrowed, hands steady, she and Hurricane thundered down the trail, faster, faster, faster. The tough bent shrubs clinging to the rocky mountain wall melded into a blur. She could hear nothing now above the whistle of the air, the laboured breathing of Hurricane and the thunder of his hooves. As they reached the final curve, Serena felt an instant's doubt. Had she, this time, gone too far? Could they, could she and Hurricane, manage the turn at this pace?

Then, oh good horse, good horse, they plunged out onto the broad level sweep of plain with Castle Rock gleaming a hard red in the distance. Serena laughed aloud and shook her head and her long silky black hair blew back from her face. Her green eyes shone with excitement and triumph. Gradually, she reined Hurricane in. What fun, what incredible fun.

Jed pulled even with her and Hurricane and Chieftain slowed together. Serena flashed Jed a blithe smile but he scowled in return. As the horses, their necks and flanks stained with sweat, slowed to a trot, he asked angrily, "Are you crazy?"

Her heart began to race. He had been so aloof until now, so perfectly the new employee. Oh, she had his attention now. She liked the way anger lighted up his startlingly blue eyes and the furious pace had ruffled his thick black hair and brought a flush to his darkly tanned face.

She laughed. "Don't you like to live dangerously, Jed?"

He stared at her, then, abruptly, without warning, he reached out and pulled her close to him and kissed her as violently as she had ridden down the trail. Hurricane and Chieftain moved uneasily against each other and Hurricane gave a low whinny.

Serena, surprised, then delighted, welcomed the pressure of his lips on hers, the hard feel of his hands against her shoulders.

He released her abruptly and pulled away on Chieftain. His blue eyes still glinted with anger. "You could have killed yourself. And Hurricane, too," he said accusingly.

Serena smiled again. "I have a lot of confidence in Hurricane—and myself."

"Do you always take such damn fool chances?" he demanded.

The horses were walking now, weary after their hard ride. Serena urged Hurricane into the lead.

She took her time answering. It seemed important to her suddenly to answer truthfully. She didn't want there to be artifice between them. Not now. Not ever. She looked back and, for an instant, remembered last summer and Peter. Peter had attracted her, too. But this time it was different. Jed was different. What was it about Jed that gave him an aura so distinctly different from anyone she had ever known? Was it the easy way he lounged in his saddle? The way his faded

Levis and worn flannel shirt fitted his lean body? The intent look in his eyes when she came near?

She felt confused suddenly. It was none of these. Or all of them. Or was it, really, the workings of her own desire, investing this handsome stranger with qualities of power and grace? Was it, she wondered brutally, the fact that he was here, an undeniably attractive man, and she was so lonely?

But, whatever there was going to be between them, let it begin honestly.

"I'm afraid," she said slowly, "that I do take chances. Always." Her green eyes looked at him gravely. "Is that . . . such a bad thing, Jed?"

Then Uncle Dan caught up with them and they were once again Jed Shelton, the new hand, and Serena Mallory, the young and lovely ward of Dan McIntire, owner of the magnificent Castle Rock ranch.

Dan McIntire dominated the barren country. He rode a huge coal black horse and the two of them threw a massive moving shadow against the sandy dusty ground. McIntire's face was rugged, worn and seamed by summer suns and winter winds. He was frowning as he looked toward Serena.

"A little too fast there, honey."

"Hurricane was born to race."

"Not down a canyon trail."

"Hurricane knows the way."

"Even a smart horse can make a mistake."

Serena knew the best defence. "Now Uncle Dan," she chided, "you are a great one to give advice about horses. Everybody in the county has warned you about Senator." As she spoke she looked at her uncle's horse. Senator moved jerkily under tight rein. His eyes rolled. He was, everyone knew, a dangerous undependable beast so why was Dan McIntire so stubborn about him?

Uncle Dan knew the best defence, too. "Oh, get along with you, Serena. I've managed Senator for ten years now." He looked down grimly at the big horse beneath him, black ears flattened. "Senator and I have an understanding. I'm boss."

"Well, you'd better never let him forget it," she said lightly, then she dug her boots into Hurricane and they surged ahead of the men. "Are we almost there?"

"Just about," Jed replied.

The little party broke into a trot, clattering across the cactus-studded plain. A half-mile ahead they could see the immense jagged mound of red rock, curved and crenellated into a thousand exotic shapes, that gave the ranch its name, Castle Rock.

"It was at the north end. I saw it yesterday from the plane," Jed explained. "It's damn strange."

They rode three abreast now and Dan McIntire was looking up toward the mass of rock. "Is there anything more beautiful in the world?" he asked, his deep voice soft.

It didn't require an answer. This was Dan McIntire's world, the rugged emptiness of New Mexico, where the sun burns high in a sky that seems to stretch to infinity, lighting the earth in delicate colours, tan and beige merging into camel, and yellows so pale they shimmer like silk.

Serena too looked up toward Castle Rock. She felt a burst of happiness. Could there ever be a happier day? To ride, the light warm breeze stirring her hair, with two men who in sharply different ways pleased her so, to be young and free, at home in a world she understood. She wished, suddenly, that this morning could go on forever, nothing changing. She reached out, gently touched her uncle's arm. "Oh, it is lovely, isn't it?"

She was so glad she had accompanied them this morning

although the object of their ride didn't interest her. Why should she care about an odd pile of stones that Jed had noticed from the air? He had been up in the Aerocommander, the five-passenger single engine plane her uncle used to keep tabs on the herds. It was another plus for Jed that he could pilot the plane.

"There are two of them," Jed was repeating, "one just at the base of Castle Rock and the other about a hundred and fifty yards due east."

But, when they reached the first stone pattern, even Serena was intrigued.

"Really, Uncle Dan," she exclaimed, "this is strange."

Dan McIntire sat astride Senator and stared down at the neatly piled stones with a puzzled frown.

Someone, and this was obviously the work of human hands, had taken stones, most of them nearly the size of a softball, and arranged them in two diagonal lines that crossed at midpoint to make an X almost fifteen feet tall.

"The other one," and Jed waved his hand to the east, "is just like this."

"Two Xs," Serena murmured. "Whatever for?"

"I don't know," Dan McIntire said slowly, "but I don't like it."

"There are Navajos . . ." Jed began, but the older man shook his head.

"No. There wouldn't be any reason." McIntire turned and looked back across the flat country. Nothing moved in the bright morning sun and the land stretched away for miles, only an occasional seguro cactus breaking the horizon. "But there are always eyes on the desert. I'll ask Joe to send out the word, ask if anyone's seen any strangers."

Joe Walkingstick had worked for her uncle as long as Serena could remember. Joe and his wife, Millie, had been so gentle and welcoming to the orphaned child who came to the ranch to stay when she was only twelve years old.

Jed was off Chieftain now, kneeling beside the foot of the X, picking up one of the stones. He scanned the ground. "It took a while to find stones all about the same size."

Senator moved restively. Uncle Dan steadied him. "It looks like some kind of marking."

Jed frowned. "Yeah. But what for? Out here in the desert with nothing but miles of emptiness. It doesn't make any sense."

"I don't like it," Dan McIntire said again, his voice a growl.

Serena understood that tone. This was McIntire land and nobody else's. Her uncle would fight about that. He didn't take trespassing lightly.

"Maybe some hunters . . ." she began.

"Not here," Uncle Dan objected. "Not unless they were after coyotes. The deer are all up in the mountains."

They left it, finally, still puzzled, but there didn't seem to be an answer.

Serena rode decorously all the way back to the hacienda, still savouring her wild descent and Jed's fiery response. He couldn't treat her so formally now. But, when they drew up at the corral and dismounted, he spoke to her uncle. "I'm going to check on the new foal."

"Good, Jed, then come on up to the house for lunch."

"Thanks, Mr. McIntire, but I believe I'll eat with the hands. I want to hear what they found in the Big East," and he smiled and rode off.

McIntire looked after him in surprise. "It's not often that anyone turns down one of Millie's lunches. That's a different young man."

"Yes," Serena agreed drily. She was quite sure she understood Jed's skittishness but she certainly had no intention of explaining to Uncle Dan.

"I like that young man," Uncle Dan continued forcefully. "I'm glad he's staying with us. Of course, I don't know how long that will last. It was a lucky day for us when his car broke down."

As they walked up the gravelled path toward the hacienda, Serena remembered the spring evening two months ago when Jed had walked up to the front door, a duffel bag slung over his shoulder. She had looked at him in surprise when she answered the front door. The hacienda was thirty miles from a narrow state highway that linked them, after another twenty miles, to Santa Fe.

He had smiled. "My car's given out on me. Would you have a phone I could use?"

"Really?" She had paused. "Were you coming here?"

"No. I'm afraid I'm lost. I was looking for a ghost town, Los Miros, and I must have taken the wrong road."

"Yes," she agreed equably, "you must have." Los Miros was forty miles in the opposite direction.

The upshot was that he stayed for dinner and, the next day, Dan McIntire flew him into Albuquerque to get parts for his car. But Jed admired the ranch so much and talked about when he had worked on ranches in Texas and been so knowledgeable that Uncle Dan asked him if he'd like to stay awhile, the spring roundup was coming up and he needed more men . . .

Yes, it was certainly a lucky day when Jed's car broke down . . .

Uncle Dan pulled open the huge wooden door of the hacienda. As Serena stepped inside, she shivered. It was always so cold when you first came in. The twelve-inch walls held the cool in summer and the heat in winter. Still, it was chilling to step from bright sunshine into shadow.

A door slammed upstairs and boot heels thudded loudly on the broad curving stairway that led down to the entry hall.

"Grandad, hey Grandad, why didn't you take me?"

Danny jumped the last half-dozen steps. Dan McIntire swept him up in his arms, smiling. "You were up too late last night, Danny, when Jenny foaled."

"Aw, Grandad, I could have gotten up. I love to go to Castle Rock. And you took Serena and she was up late, too."

"I don't need as much sleep as a growing boy," Serena said quickly.

Danny wriggled out of his grandfather's arms, still looking unhappy.

Dan slipped an arm around Danny's thin shoulders. "I'll tell you what, Danny, you and I will take a ride to Castle Rock next week. We'll have Millie pack us a big picnic lunch and I'll show you the trail that crosses the ranch near Castle Rock and . . ."

Serena followed them into the dining room, smiling at the two of them, Uncle Dan so huge and Danny so little. Danny would be ten in the fall. He was small for his age, slightly built and not very robust, rather like his mother. Serena remembered Claire as a gentle and delicate woman with a quiet smile. Danny's father had been cheerfully loud and vigorous.

Serena's smile slipped away. When she remembered Danny's parents, she recalled her own mother and father, Tom and Kitty Mallory. She carried in her mind a very clear memory of that last day when her mother said goodbye to her, "You'll have fun visiting the ranch, sweetie. Daddy and I will be back next week."

They had gone as guests on Dan Jr.'s yacht and an unex-

14

pected storm struck the Gulf. They found pieces of *The Sand Castle* for the next several weeks but no survivors. Serena Mallory, age twelve, had no other living relatives, nowhere to go, no one to take her. She marvelled again at Dan McIntire's great heart. He made nothing of it. Castle Rock would be her home, though she was only the daughter of friends with no call of kinship. Castle Rock would always be her home.

Serena slipped into her place at the huge mahogany table. The table seemed even larger with only a few of them to eat. It was more of a size when the season began for Castle Rock was not only a working ranch but, during the summer, a dude ranch. It always surprised Serena that Uncle Dan had opened the ranch to vacationers even though the visitors were a small group. Perhaps it helped ease the pain he must have felt when his only son was killed and there were suddenly so many empty places at his table. It was the next summer after *The Sand Castle* went down that four cabins were built among the fir trees in the high ground that rose behind the hacienda. She and Will and Julie had always looked forward to the coming of summer for there would be new faces and new friends. The ranch gained a quiet reputation among travel agents and there was always a long list of applicants.

But now she and Uncle Dan and Danny took their places at one end of the long table. The guests would not begin to arrive for another week.

Uncle Dan looked across the table at Serena and frowned. "Where's Will?"

"Perhaps he didn't hear the bell, Uncle Dan," Serena said quickly. "I'll go see." She started to push back her chair, wondering as she did why she continued to have an impulse to protect Will. He had heard the bell, of course. How could he have missed it? And he knew that Uncle Dan expected promptness at meals. It was a small thing, but to Dan

15

McIntire a courtesy to be expected, especially when the dudes came.

Then Will appeared in the doorway, his red hair tousled, his blue eyes vague. "Sorry I'm late. In the middle of . . . Well, anyway, sorry," and he hurried awkwardly to his place.

He was, Serena thought, so big that he stumbled over himself. It was odd that those massive hands could wield a paintbrush so delicately, creating paintings with a clarity and grace that each time surprised her. And his blue eyes, now so vague, must in reality see more than most ever did of the incredible variations in colour that made the New Mexico landscape so hauntingly different.

As Will sat down, he looked towards her and his gaze was so openly adoring that Serena felt sad.

She wished things could be different. She did love Will— like a brother. And that's all there was to it.

She smiled at him and abruptly his face lit up. As Millie brought in their lunch, he leaned close to Serena. "I've got some things I'd like to show you, some things I've just done."

"I'd like to see them, Will."

"Maybe after lunch . . ."

Then Uncle Dan broke in, "Oh Will, I've been meaning to check with you. The phone bill shows a half dozen calls from the ranch to New York. Serena said she hadn't made them. I think there's been some mistake and . . ."

"Oh." Will hesitated then shook his head. "No. It's not a mistake."

Uncle Dan looked surprised. "Oh, well, of course, if you made them, that's fine."

Will tugged at his thick reddish beard. "Yeah, I've talked to New York a lot lately." He flushed. "Thing about it is, I may be able to set up a show there."

16

"In New York?" Uncle Dan asked interestedly.

Will nodded slowly.

Serena felt sure suddenly that Will was lying. She had known Will for so long, he and Julie. She knew them . . . Serena put down her fork, reached for her ice water to try and ease the dryness in her throat. Before last summer, she would have said she knew Will and Julie so well that nothing they ever did could surprise her.

But had Julie's actions really surprised her, a small cold voice asked within. She knew Julie, yes. Beautiful Julie, so small and delicate and blonde, with a kind of beauty that took your breath away. But Serena knew what lay behind that lovely face and bubbly smile, knew the childlike self-interest that could be so shocking. Was it any wonder that Julie had thrown herself at Peter?

Serena drank but the tight ache in her throat didn't ease.

Almost. That was a word to conjure with. Lost kingdoms, lost lives, lost loves. It hardly did to cling to almost. And didn't it mean, really, that Peter was not the man for her?

But Serena had thought he was and that was what hurt so much. And made her wary now. Made her wonder if she could ever be sure of . . . anyone. In her mind, she could see Jed so clearly, the look of pleasure in his eyes when she came near.

"Serena, don't you think that's right?"

She looked blankly at Will, realizing she hadn't heard a word he had said, but his expression was so familiar. It was the same look he had given her through the years when he was out of his depth and needed help.

"Oh, I agree, Will, I certainly do," she said quickly.

His blue eyes smiled at her then he looked back at his uncle.

17

Dan McIntire was nodding slowly. "I can see the justice of what you say, Will, and we shouldn't stand in the way of science. But I've never wanted to have a lot of strangers roaming around the ranch. Of course, these archaeologists could learn a lot from our ruins . . ."

Serena smiled to herself. Her uncle was so fiercely possessive of Castle Rock Ranch, even to the point of calling the Anasazi ruins 'our' ruins. They had been there, of course, long before the first Europeans entered the desert and mesa and mountain country peopled by the Pueblo Indians. The Anasazi were American's first apartment dwellers, their adobe complexes built into sweeping curves in the sides of golden sandstone cliffs from AD 700 to 1300, safe from foes and predators. The great culture waned after 1300, brought down, many archaeologists believed, by drought, still New Mexico's greatest enemy. The Castle Rock ruins, unspoiled and untouched, attracted many archaeologists but Uncle Dan had refused to permit excavations. Serena realized that Will, desperate to steer the conversation away from himself and the telephone calls to New York, must have suggested that Uncle Dan change his mind. It was a sure-fire way to distract him.

". . . might let some of them dig if they promised not to do any damage." Dan McIntire frowned down at his plate. "I just don't know, Will, but I'll think about it." His troubled gaze moved to Serena. "Do you think it would be a good thing, Serry?"

She felt a rush of love for him as he called her by the childhood nickname. Uncle Dan was so good and he tried so hard to always do the right thing, to them, to the land, to the people of his stark, yet magnificent country. She hesitated. "I think," she said gently, "that it would be all right, Uncle Dan. We could be very particular about who we permitted to come and for how long. And we could insist that they not disturb the old burial grounds. It could be arranged so that no harm would be done."

They were still talking about it, listing the pros and cons, when Millie brought in dessert, pineapple sherbet, and announced, "There is a long-distance call, Mr. McIntire."

When he had left the dining room, Serena turned to Will. "Who are you calling in New York, darling? The Mafia?"

Will hunched his shoulders and didn't look at her. "Oh no, no, just a gallery, a fellow I met at a show last year in Santa Fe. You know the kind of thing."

His voice was so evasive that Serena felt more certain than ever that the art show was a lie from beginning to end. She frowned. Will looked strained and tired.

"Will, what's wrong?" she asked suddenly.

"Nothing."

"Will, I know you," she said gently. "Please, let me help. Whatever it is."

He did look at her then and the pain in his eyes shocked her.

"I can't tell you," he began and then the dining room door opened. "Shh. Here comes Uncle Dan."

Dan McIntire was smiling as he sat down. "Good news, you two, Julie's coming home."

For an instant, Will and Serena turned frozen faces to him, both of them, Serena realized oddly, caught up in shock. But why, she wondered, should Will feel this way? He had always followed where Julie led. Will adored his sister.

Uncle Dan dipped into his sherbet, too busy talking to see their reaction. "I'll fly into Albuquerque and pick them up. Their flight gets in at four tomorrow . . ."

Serena managed a smile and said, she hoped, the right things.

They. Of course. Julie and her new husband, Peter.

How in the world could she bear it?

# Two

"Are you sure you won't come, Serena?"

Serena stood by the driver's door of the jeep. She bent and kissed her uncle on the cheek. "No, it would make the plane so crowded. And you know Julie will have a lot of luggage."

Dan McIntire smiled. "That's true enough. I'll give Julie your love."

"Do that," Serena replied. "And I'll be here when you get back."

When the dust rose after the jeep on its way to the single lane airstrip south of the hacienda, Serena jammed her hands in the back pockets of her Levis and slowly walked back toward the front steps.

You can do what you have to do. She had learned that as a small child. She would manage. And surely Julie and Peter would not stay very long. Serena paused and looked up at the hacienda, its adobe gleaming like soft gold in the afternoon sunlight. What had Julie called it once? A clay mausoleum. But not, of course, in front of Uncle Dan.

Silence cloaked the huge house like the first snowfall high in the mountains. Serena paused in the entryway then turned and walked through the shadowy living room with its ranch furniture and pots of ferns toward the office that opened out of the den. Since she had returned to Castle Rock from college, she had spent almost every afternoon typing letters and keeping accounts for her uncle.

She suspected it was his kindly way of making her a part of the pulse of the working ranch. She did a good job, always careful to produce perfect letters and accurate entries in the ledger. She was gaining a clearer picture of the complexity of running a huge ranch with 10,000 head of cattle. Always there was the worry about water and whether there would be enough and how to maintain the herds when water ran short as it so often did. She'd learned how to keep feed available during the harsh winter months and when to move the herds to follow the grasses. She'd learned when to cull and brand, when to ship, when to sell and when to hold. And, of course, there was all the extra planning involved to take care of the summer dudes.

It would be a lot for Danny to master someday.

Someday . . .

She laid down her pen and the figures merged into a blur of meaningless shapes.

She couldn't stay at Castle Rock forever.

It hurt to think it. It hurt all the way through. She loved the ranch, the clear brilliant days, the silent nights with stars in shiny silver clusters. She loved the unexpected glimpses of life in the brown and dusty countryside, the flicker of a rabbit's tail, the tawny pelt of a coyote sliping up an arroyo, the sturdy seguro cactus with its surprising flowers in the spring.

She was here now. Enjoy the moment, Serena told herself. No one can be sure of tomorrow. Enjoy today.

She pushed back her chair. She had the mid-afternoon blahs, not helped at all by the tension that tightened her shoulders as the time drew nearer and nearer for Julie and Peter to arrive. Serena decided to go to the kitchen. There were always luscious things in Millie's kitchen. Today was no exception. Fresh butterscotch brownies sat on a blue plate.

Raspberry oatmeal cookies cooled on wire racks.

Serena was smiling as she sat down with a cookie and a tall glass of icy milk. It would be all right. She was over Peter Carey. Definitely over Peter. He could not possibly have been the right man for her, not if he truly enjoyed the life he and Julie led, living in Manhattan, and spending leisure time in Monte Carlo and Acapulco. This would be their first visit to Castle Rock since their marriage last summer. Serena could not imagine staying away from New Mexico for a year. So, it would be all right. She and Julie would be just as they always had been.

Finishing her snack, she took the plate and glass to the sink to rinse, then pushed through the kitchen door which swung noiselessly on its hinges. She took a step or two into the dining room then stopped and lifted her head to listen.

The house was so still, the quiet of siesta. Millie always went to her cabin for siesta. Joe, of course, would be out on the ranch. In any event, he would never be upstairs. Only the family or Millie would be upstairs. And the noise came from upstairs.

Serena walked slowly forward to look up the shadowy reaches of the curving stairway.

Uncle Dan and Danny and Will had flown to Albuquerque. Only she had remained here at the house, the house now so quiet during siesta.

Again, so clearly and unmistakably, Serena heard footsteps.

Serena swung to her left. It took her only a moment to slip through the dim living room to the great brick fireplace and the gun rack beside it. She reached up, found the key on the ledge, opened the glass case and lifted out the Winchester repeating rifle. She checked the magazine, made sure the safety catch was on, then turned back the way she had come.

23

She crept up the stairway. The noise of the intruder was unmistakable when she reached the second floor landing. Uncle Dan's room was at the head of the stairs. His door was closed as was Serena's and the room that would be Julie's and Peter's.

But Will's door was ajar. Within, someone opened and closed drawers.

Serena hesitated.

Could Will have returned before the others?

No, there wasn't any way. And, if all of them had returned, she would have been caught up in the bustle of Julie's home-coming.

The rifle heavy in her hands, Serena took one step then another nearer Will's door. She kept to the Navajo rug in the centre of the hall to deaden her footsteps. She edged up to Will's half-open door and looked inside. Her breath caught in her throat.

He stood with his back to the door but she couldn't mistake him, not the broad sweep of his shoulders, his lean hips and legs. He stood, hands on his hips, looking carefully around the room.

"Jed!" The shocked exclamation escaped her without thought.

For an instant, just an instant, and later she would wonder if she imagined it, his body tensed, then, quickly, easily, he swung around, smiling, "Serena, maybe you can . . ." He stopped, staring at the rifle. "For heaven's sake, Serena, what's the artillery for?"

She held the rifle loosely in her hands. "I heard a noise. I thought everyone was gone."

"Hey," and he crossed to her, put a hand on her arm, " I'm sorry. I didn't mean to frighten you. I thought no one was here."

Yes, she thought coldly, that is what you must have thought, that you had the house to yourself.

But he was turning toward the bookcase. "Maybe you can help me, Serena. Will said I could borrow his book on Peter Hurd. I was trying to find it. I've looked everywhere but I don't see it. Do you?"

"It's downstairs."

"Downstairs! Why, I thought . . . but I must have misunderstood Will."

"Do you mean the big book with a collection of Hurd's paintings?" Serena asked.

"Yes, that's the one."

"It's in the living room on the rosewood table next to the organ."

Jed carried the rifle downstairs for her, chatting companionably. She found the book for him and he took it with thanks, then helped her replace the rifle in the cabinet. As she locked the case, he was looking at the collection.

"Your uncle has some nice guns there."

"Yes. They're worth a good deal."

If he noticed the dry tone in her voice, he gave no sign of it. In fact, he shook his head. "I didn't mean what they're worth. Just that they are good guns. Does he hunt much?"

Serena shook her head. "Not as much as he did when Dan Jr. was alive."

"Dan Jr.?"

So Serena told him of the long-ago accident.

"That must have been a great tragedy in his life," Jed said quietly.

"Yes. But at least he has Danny."

Jed leaned casually against the organ, holding the heavy book in his hands. He looked at her quizzically, "And he has you, Serena."

He had in the last few weeks become so much a part of the ranch day, riding out in the mornings with Joe to supervise the hands, taking up the Aerocommander to check on the herds, that it came as a surprise to realize how little, really, he knew of them.

"I meant real family," she explained, "when I mentioned Danny."

"Real family? But I thought . . . Aren't you his niece? A brother or sister's daughter?"

She smiled. "No. Actually, I'm Uncle Dan's ward. He always told me to call him Uncle. I think he did it to make me feel more secure. You see, my parents were friends of Dan Jr.'s and were lost in the storm, too. I've lived here ever since, except when I was away at school."

"I see," Jed said slowly. "So you aren't any relation at all. Then what about Will and Julie?"

"They are his nephew and niece, the children of his sister, Jessica."

"Is she dead, too?"

Idly Serena fiddled with the cover of the organ. How to explain Jessica? There was scarcely any way.

"Jessica's not the sort to stay on a ranch," Serena began. "She's . . . international. She loves Paris and San Francisco and Rome. She's been married at least four times and right now I think she's living on a Greek island with a French film star."

Jed gave a soft whistle. "I know Castle Rock's a big ranch but I wouldn't have thought it would run to that kind of money."

"Oh, it doesn't. Uncle Dan's very rigid about some things, one of which is Jessica. She dumped the kids on him when they were little and she occasionally drops in for a visit, but she doesn't get a penny out of Castle Rock. He gave her a settlement years ago with the understanding that she would never make a claim for the ranch."

"How does she manage the jet set life style?"

Serena smiled slightly. "She's very beautiful. Still. And she rarely marries a poor man."

"And this Julie who's coming today, she's Jessica's daughter?"

Serena's smile faded. "Right."

Jed looked at her curiously. "You don't like her much?"

"Julie and Will and I grew up together."

"That doesn't answer my question."

"No."

It was his turn to smile a little. "I like you when you are angry. You remind me of a black cat, ready to run or fight."

"I don't usually run."

"Is that why you stayed home this afternoon?"

"I have no quarrel with Julie."

"No?"

"No."

"Then tell me about her."

She could have slapped him, but that would be a betrayal too. Instead, she lifted her chin. "Julie . . . why, she's Jessica's daughter. Beautiful. Appealing. Bewitching, actually. You'll see when you meet her."

"Is she rich, too?"

The question caught her a little by surprise. But then everything with Jed this afternoon had been unexpected, finding him in Will's room and now this conversation with its odd turns.

"No. Julie and Will don't have any money. Their father caroused through all of his and went bankrupt before he died. And Jessica would never dream of sharing."

27

"So what does Julie do?"

"She lives in New York with her husband. When they aren't on the Riviera."

"What does he do?"

"Oh, I don't know," Serena said vaguely. "He has investments of some kind."

"Hmm, they sound like interesting people." Then he raised his head. "I hear the plane now. I'll excuse myself, Serena, I don't want to intrude on your reunion."

"You won't intrude."

He smiled. "No, this isn't the time for a ranch hand to hang around. I'm sure there will be a lot of visiting you will want to do."

She wondered, as the door closed behind him, whether there had been irony in his voice. Then, as the roar of the plane came nearer, she took a deep breath and walked toward the door.

Serena was waiting with a smile when the jeep pulled up in front of the broad adobe steps. Julie swept towards her and she was, of course, lovely in an ice-blue silk dress that looked fresh and perfect as if it had just that moment been taken from a cachet-lined closet.

They brushed cheeks and Serena caught the delicate scent of Halston.

Julie stepped back a little, still clasping Serena's hands.

"My dear, you look wonderful. Peter, look how gloriously healthy Serena looks."

Serena abruptly felt terribly conscious of her faded jeans and plain cotton blouse.

Damn Julie.

She looked past Julie toward Peter and, for a dreadful instant, it was a year ago and he was climbing out of the jeep, a guest scheduled for a two-week visit. He had been then, as

28

now, incredibly handsome, his blond hair shining like wheat in the sun, his blue eyes friendly and smiling. Then the moments rushed together and she held out her hand, "Hello, Peter, it's good to see you again."

"Hi, Serena." His hand was warm and firm. "Looks like you've kept the home fires burning."

Suddenly, it was easy. She led the way up the steps and said good-humouredly over her shoulder, "Oh, we manage to keep things going. How long can you and Julie stay?"

"A few weeks. We're having our apartment redone. Besides, New York is an oven in the summer."

"It's fairly warm here," she said drily.

"Oh well, the mountains and all."

She remembered then that he had surprised her last summer, he spent so much time riding out alone.

Julie dropped her purse on the sideboard in the foyer and clapped her hands. "Oh Uncle Dan, it's good to be home. I've been looking forward to it so much."

Uncle Dan came up behind her, carrying some bags.

"Oh, don't bring those in here, Uncle Dan. Peter and I will stay in Greenbrier."

Greenbrier was the largest and finest of the guest quarters.

Uncle Dan was already starting up the stairs. He paused. "Sorry, Julie, but Greenbrier is for guests. Millie's busy freshening up all the cabins this week. The first dudes will come in this weekend. Millie has your old room all ready for you and Peter."

Will and Danny were just coming in the front door with more luggage. Only Serena could see Peter's face. He was scowling. He looked at his wife and jerked his head up toward Uncle Dan's retreating back. Julie made a little face and spread her hands as if to say, I can't help it. Then the moment was past as Peter turned, smiling, to Will, and reached out to take a suitcase, and Julie started up the stairs.

Serena stood in the entry way, a puzzled look on her face.

# Three

The week whirled past and, almost before Serena had time to make half the necessary arrangements, the first summer guests arrived. Uncle Dan stood at the top of the steps with Serena and Julie, and Will and Peter ranged behind him.

Jed came around to open the door of the ranch's VW bus. "Let me help you, Mrs. Minter," and he reached up to give his hand to the most languorous looking blonde Serena had ever seen. Although Serena was schooled enough not to change expression, she thought, wow, what a summer this is going to be. Mr. Minter followed and Serena wondered what travel agent had sent this couple to a dude ranch. Howard Minter's face was flushed red from whisky. He wore a tight plaid suit and three rings on his right hand.

The second couple off the bus, the Rhodes, were typical dudes, wiry and athletic people in their thirties with three lively children.

Two men, John Morris and George VanZandt, completed the party. Serena liked them immediately. Morris was short and stocky with a cheerful open face. VanZandt was tall and lean and looked like he would be more at home in Levis than in his cord suit.

Will helped the Minters with their luggage and led the way to Greenbrier. Jed balanced tennis rackets and duffel bags and took the Rhodes in tow. They were assigned to Azul cabin.

31

Serena greeted the two men. "I'm Serena Mallory and I hope you both find your stay at Castle Rock to be pleasant. If you'll follow me, I'll take you to your cabin. It's just a brief walk this way, up among the pines," and they set out for Desperado Point. "I hope you don't mind that your cabin is a bit farther than the others."

The two men kept up with her easily even though they were wearing city shoes and must have found the path with its uneven blanket of pine needles a little slippery.

"No, this will suit us perfectly, Miss Mallory," John Morris said. His voice was deep and clear. "George and I are working together on a book and that's why we've chosen Castle Rock for our vacation. Our wives are visiting their families and this will give us a chance to compare the drafts we've worked on this winter. And if our cabin is out of the way, so much the better. Then our typewriters won't disturb any of the other guests."

Serena looked at him with interest. "What kind of book are you writing?"

VanZandt smiled. "I'm afraid you're going to be disappointed, Miss Mallory. We're working on a physics text."

"Oh." To tell the truth, she was disappointed. She had been excited at the prospect of meeting authors. "I'm sure that must be very interesting," she said quickly.

Both of them laughed. "I can tell," VanZandt said pleasantly, "that western hospitality is alive and thriving at Castle Rock."

As she unlocked the door to their cabin and turned on the lights, Serena replied, "That is one thing you certainly don't have to worry about at Castle Rock."

She explained how the wall heater worked as the nights could be quite cold, showed them the extra blankets, how to dial the house should they need anything and told them dinner would be at six-thirty in the big dining room at the hacienda. "We stock the kitchenettes and leave breakfast up to the guests. As for lunch, we will either have a meal in the main house or there will be box lunches to take if you go on any of the outings."

"Outings?" Morris asked.

"Oh yes, we plan rides two or three times a week, either up into the mountains or out to Castle Rock," and she described the huge rock that had given the ranch its name. "And we have two tennis courts, a putting green and a swimming pool."

"There are some ruins, aren't there?" VanZandt inquired.

Serena nodded slowly. "Yes, but we don't show them. Mr. McIntire doesn't usually permit anyone to visit the ruins. We had trouble one summer with some guests who . . . well, they treated it like a souvenir hunt, and he is quite determined to protect them. We'll see."

"Oh, that's all right," Morris said quickly. "George and I will probably just ride out a bit by ourselves as we have so much to discuss. We wouldn't have time for any long-range trip to the ruins, anyway. And, if you don't usually show them, we certainly wouldn't expect any special treatment."

Serena smiled warmly at them.

As she walked back down to the hacienda, she thought how nice it was to have guests who didn't expect special treatment. She had a feeling the Minters wouldn't share that philosophy.

Serena was right.

By the end of the week, Serena's immediate response, when the red signal light flickered on her desk phone, was a scowl. That had never before been a byproduct of their guests, but Mrs. Minter was impossible. And Julie wasn't any help. Julie wandered restlessly around the house when Uncle

Dan and Jed were out and Peter spent his time practicing golf shots on the practice tee and taking occasional long rides.

Serena glared at the phone as it buzzed again.

"Hello, Serena here."

"Oh, Serena," Mrs. Minter snapped, "I wish you would do something about that little boy. He's waked me up again."

Serena glanced at the desk clock. Eleven-fifteen. God. "I'm sorry," she said pleasantly, "I'll talk to Danny."

"It's that damned horse of his. It makes so much noise."

Serena drew her breath. "Perhaps if you took some riding lessons, you might feel . . ."

"Riding lessons! I wouldn't get up on one of those brutes for anything!"

Serena almost asked why in the hell she had come to Castle Rock, but she didn't. Uncle Dan always insisted that all guests be treated with the utmost courtesy. It had never before, Serena thought, been so hard.

"I'm sorry you feel that way," Serena said, still pleasantly. "We would like for you to enjoy your stay here."

"Yeah. Well, thanks. Look, why don't you come over and have a drink."

So far this week, Lou Minter had treated Serena on a par with a hotel maid. This request must mean that the woman was dreadfully lonely—or bored. But Serena felt there was a limit to what Uncle Dan would expect.

"I'm sorry, I wish I could but I have to help put the box lunches together then I'm taking the Rhodes on a ride to Missionary Lake."

"Oh."

Serena glimpsed Julie walking down the hall. "I'll tell you what, Mrs. Minter, why don't I see if Julie could come. I imagine . . ."

34

"Oh no, that's all right. I'll take a bath," and the phone clicked into the cradle.

Serena shrugged. Now that was odd. She would have supposed that Mrs. Minter would feel an instinctive bond with Julie who wore such gorgeous, expensive and absolutely non-ranch wear clothes, and who was, so obviously to everyone but Uncle Dan, bored out of her mind. Instead Mrs. Minter had jumped back as if Serena had suggested a *tete à tete* with a nun.

"Damned if I understand anybody," Serena muttered.

She slapped the receiver down and hurried to the kitchen. She did have box lunches to fix and it seemed there was never enough time to get everything done now that the season had started.

The afternoon, spent with the congenial and appreciative Rhodes, restored her usual good humour. They rode up to the lake which was deep and still and cold and ate lunch on a huge slab of red rock and watched the children toss rocks down into the water. Serena especially enjoyed seeing Danny have such a good time with the Rhodes children. It reminded her of those long-ago days when she and Will and Julie had raced up and down mountain trails and never worried about tomorrow.

She was rather quiet on the ride back down the mountain. Why had she thought of it like that? Remembered with pleasure those days because they hadn't worried about tomorrow. Was she worried now?

A white tail deer flashed by among the pines to their left. Serena reined up and called to the others. But underneath, the thought kept pulling and tugging. Was she worried?

Not, she thought, precisely worried. But something was wrong, something at Castle Rock, and what really bothered her was the fact that she had no idea what was making her feel that way.

Back at the corral, Serena supervised as the Rhodes and their children unsaddled the horses, rubbed them down and fed them.

After the others had gone, Serena lingered in the tack room. She took her time putting away the saddle blankets and hanging the bridles and bits. Then, with a thrill of excitement, she heard the sound of Jed's voice as he called to someone. When he came into the tack room, carrying his gear, she was at work mending a bridle.

"Still at it, Serena?"

"Just finishing up. I took the Rhodes up to Missionary Lake today. What did you do?"

"We rounded up some stragglers in Glen Valley and took them back to the main herd."

"I believe I'd take that over the tourists."

He looked at her in surprise. "I thought the Rhodes seemed like nice people."

"Oh, they are," Serena said quickly. "It's some of the others."

"The Minters?"

She nodded. "Not hard to guess, is it?"

"Where are they from?" he asked casually.

"LA. Wouldn't you know it?"

"Yeah. You'd think Vegas would be more to their taste."

"Oh, it is, it is. I've heard all about the Sands and Frankie and Della."

He grinned. "How did they happen to come here?"

"I can't imagine," Serena said wearily. "Maybe they're on the lam."

Jed hung up his saddle then turned back to face her. "Seriously, Serena, how do you suppose they ever heard of Castle Rock?"

"Maybe they thought we were a cruise ship."

36

Jed laughed but he persisted. "No, look at it. They had to know where they were coming. Why don't you talk to her, see if you can find out why they came here."

"I'd rather talk to a hooded cobra."

Jed laughed again.

Serena finished with the bridle, hung it and turned toward the door. Jed came with her. As they stepped out into the bright sunshine, she said, "If you want to, you can talk to her yourself tonight."

"Tonight?"

"You are coming, aren't you?" she asked, suddenly breathless. "We always have what Uncle Dan calls a social every Friday night during the summer. All the guests are invited and the family and you, too, of course."

"I'm just a hired hand."

"Uncle Dan said he especially wanted you to come." He hadn't, but he would, Serena knew, be pleased.

"In that event, I'll come," Jed said easily. "I'll look forward to it."

And Serena looked forward to the evening, too.

This first social of the summer was going to be especially festive. Serena had worked all week, making the arrangements, making sure there were plenty of country and western tapes for the stereo, including, of course, the Texas two-step and San Antonio promenade. She had rearranged the furniture in the den so there would be plenty of room for dancing and stocked the bar, including Coors and wine for the ladies since Uncle Dan didn't believe in hard spirits for ladies. After Mrs. Minter discovered the bar didn't run to gin, Serena wondered how the evening would go. But that, she felt, was Mrs. Minter's problem. Probably the arrival of the neighbours would distract her. There were some very attractive men at some of the surrounding ranches.

Serena helped Millie clear the dinner dishes then checked on the *hors d'ouevres*. When everything was ready she nodded, then hurried upstairs to dress. She swept her hair back in a chignon and lightly touched her cheeks with blush. She chose a long swirling skirt but couldn't decide between a saucy peasant blouse or a more low-cut soft cotton top. Smiling, she finally slipped on the low-cut blouse and added a necklace of shining turquoise. Uncle Dan had given it to her on her twenty-first birthday. She looked into the long mirror. Her hair shone softly, the colour of a midnight sky, and the blue-green of the turquoise emphasized the vivid green of her eyes. She looked lovely and she knew it with a surge of delight. Excitement hung in the air. She had not so looked forward to an evening for a long, long time.

It began gloriously, despite the Minters. Old friends arrived in a drove, the Salazars from Circle Bar M, the Mackenzies from Burnt Hill, the Berrys from Dutchman Creek, the Montoyas from Crazy Horse. The den resounded with booming voices and laughter and lots of talk, the outlook for the fall beef prices, the battle against new federal regulations, the worry of the continuing drought, the price of feed. And the dudes mixed in, welcomed by the friendly ranch families.

Except, of course, for the Minters.

Sam Berry from Dutchman Creek took a liking to Mrs. Minter. Sam stood six feet two in his stockings and was built like a brown bear and he had a reputation as a brawler. He and Lou Minter retired to a secluded corner near the gun rack. Replenishing a relish tray near them, Serena overheard an animated discussion of the blackjack table at the Sahara. Serena glanced across the room at Sam Berry's wife, Chrissie, caught a look of weariness and felt a pang of sympathy. Why did some men have to be such asses?

Serena moved from group to group, smiling, hearing the latest gossip, and waiting for Jed to come. It was almost nine when she saw him standing a little hesitantly in the archway to the den. He wore tan slacks and a blue polo shirt open at the throat. He looked strong and confident even in this roomful of hardy men. Serena was walking toward him, smiling, but she had taken only a few steps when Julie turned and reached out to take his hand and draw him into the circle around her.

Serena stopped. Before she could move again, Howard Minter blocked her way.

"Hey there, honey, you're a real picture tonight."

Serena looked up at him blankly. But it wasn't for you, she thought, that I chose this blouse, wore my turquoise necklace.

She forced a smile. "How are you tonight, Mr. Minter?"

His heavy arm slid around her shoulders and she could smell the thick sweetness of bourbon on his breath. "Oh now, we don't have to be so formal. My name's Howard. And you're Serena. That's a pretty name."

"Thank you," she said stiffly.

"Here," and he began to steer her toward the centre of the long room and the open space where a few couples danced. "Let's get in on this number. I'm a pretty good dancer."

It would have been rude to pull away. And Serena had been taught never to be rude.

She hated the feel of his hot heavy hand on her back, and disliked being close to him, smelling the mixture of bourbon and a cloying men's cologne. Over his shoulder, she could see Julie and Jed dancing close together, looking like a couple made for each other.

A heavy sense of foreboding settled over her.

Not again. Surely not again.

Julie was laughing up at Jed, tilting her head back. Her shining blonde hair swung free, showing the graceful line of her throat and shoulder.

Lovely, lovely Julie.

When the couples turned and Jed looked across the room, Serena's face remained stolid and blank. The smile that began on his face slipped away and she had a final glimpse of surprise in his dark blue eyes.

As the couples moved in the controlled circles of the dance and again Serena and Jed faced each other, she was ready with a smile—but this time Jed was looking down at Julie, his face absorbed and intent.

The dance seemed interminable to Serena, a parody of pleasure. As the music ended, she excused herself from Howard Minter on the plea of checking the kitchen. But when she saw Jed and Julie standing close together in a little oasis of privacy at the far end of the room, Serena turned and walked blindly toward the french windows.

She slipped out into the cool darkness of the patio and walked deep into the shadows of the magnolia. The gentle night breeze rustled the glossy heavy leaves. She pressed her hands against her flaming cheeks and plunged even farther away from the brightly shining windows toward the end of the hacienda. It was quiet here, away from the rising tide of voices and music, away from Jed and Julie. Her slippers made no sound against the flagstones.

But, when she heard Uncle Dan's angry voice, raised almost to a shout, she knew he was too upset to care whether he was overheard. She had heard that kind of tone in his voice only once before, years ago. She didn't remember now why she had been present at the confrontation, she remembered only the sound of Dan McIntire's voice. A cowboy who had worked for the ranch for years had been discovered to be

40

rustling cattle, segregating them in a hidden canyon, altering their brands and spiriting them out a few at a time to sell.

Dan McIntire had been outraged. His voice had shaken with fury. "A man is either honest or he isn't."

Now, so many years later, she heard the same anguish and outrage in his voice in a scrap of a sentence.

". . . on my land?"

There was no mistaking who spoke. She would have bet her life on it.

Someone else spoke then but his voice was low and indistinguishable. She couldn't hear the words or recognize the speaker.

Then Uncle Dan spoke again, still loudly, still angrily. "Goddammit, I won't have it! I'll stop it." Then his voice lowered and she just caught a few more words, ". . . glad you told me. I'll . . ."

A door closed then and the voices were gone. Serena stood uncertainly for a moment, just outside the office window.

Something was terribly wrong.

She gathered up her skirt and began to run lightly back toward the french windows. She must find Uncle Dan, talk to him. She came back into the brightly lit room. Voices rose and fell cheerfully, music throbbed in the background. Couples danced. It was just exactly as it had been a few moments ago and that shocked Serena because she knew something was terribly wrong.

She saw Uncle Dan then. He was all the way across the room, standing in the archway to the hall, listening courteously to Rosa Montoya of Crazy Horse Ranch. But Serena thought she saw, even at this distance, a look of strain on his face.

She started across the room, but one person stopped her,

then another. From each she disengaged as quickly as possible, then, near the organ, she found her way blocked by Julie and Jed.

Serena tried to slip past. "Excuse me," she murmured.

Julie reached out a slender hand, the nails long and perfect and vividly red. "Why, Serena, where have you been? In the kitchen?"

Her lazy tone suggested that the kitchen, of course, was Serena's proper place.

Serena managed a smile. "Actually, Julie, I've been out on the patio. It's a lovely night."

"All alone?"

"That would be telling," Serena replied coolly. Then she looked directly at Jed. "Have you had a good time tonight?"

He looked from one of them to the other then said, almost angrily, "I always have a good time."

"Damn lucky. That's what you are. Damn lucky." The words were thick and slurred. "Don't have a good time. Not anymore."

The three of them turned in unison, like marionettes, to look up at Will. A very drunk Will. He swayed back and forth, from toe to heel, like a huge tree ready to topple.

Serena felt a pang of distress. Before dinner, Will had smiled at her, his light blue eyes eager, and asked her to promise him a dance. "Like old times," he had said happily. "Of course, Will," she had answered, looking forward to the evening, "it will be like old times."

And she had not looked for him, not the whole evening long. There had been the kitchen to check and old friends to greet and Jed to wait for. And now the evening was almost over and she had never danced with Will.

Will's face was puddly and slack. "No damn good," he muttered thickly, "no damn good anymore."

42

Serena looked past Will toward the archway. Uncle Dan had little patience with those who drank too much. A drunk was never invited back to Castle Rock. If he saw Will like this . . . Serena reached out, took Will's arm, "Come on," she said gently, "let's take a walk, Will."

It took Will a long moment to understand then he tried to smile. "With me, Serry, will you walk with me?"

"Of course I will. Come on now, let's go this way."

They started off toward the french windows and he leaned against her, so big and heavy. Then he stopped. "Serry," he said slowly, painfully, "you won't want to walk with me. Not anymore."

She tugged at his arm. Uncle Dan was still standing in the archway, moving now toward the foyer as some of the guests began to leave.

"Of course I'll walk with you, Will. Let's go out this way." She wanted to get him out to the patio and around the side of the house and up the outside stairs to his room. She tugged again.

Then Peter and Jed came up on either side.

"Come on, old man," Peter said briskly, "we'll give you a hand."

Will stiffened and tried to pull his arms free but the two men were moving him ahead now.

"We'll take care of him," Jed said quietly. "You and Julie go ahead and help say goodbye to the guests."

Serena hesitated but Jed and Peter had Will to the window now, then Will looked back and his face was so sorrowful that Serena took a step after them.

"Oh come on, Serena," Julie said irritably. "They'll see to him."

"But Julie, what can be the matter? What's wrong with Will?"

43

"Nothing," she snapped. "He's drunk. The fool." And her face was white and angry. Her hand caught Serena's elbow and the two of them turned toward the archway.

"Don't tell Uncle Dan," Julie said in a low tight voice.

"Of course not," Serena replied angrily. Julie didn't have to tell her that.

Then they were caught up in the knot of guests and dudes saying good night. When the front door finally shut behind the last of them, the smile faded from Uncle Dan's face and he looked stern and sombre.

Serena wanted to ask him what was wrong but Julie was standing beside him and she slipped a hand through his arm and turned and walked with him toward the stairs. Serena trailed along behind.

"Another successful dance at Castle Rock," Julie said lightly.

Uncle Dan looked down as if just realizing she walked with him. Then he managed to smile. "Did you have a good time, honey?"

"Oh, a wonderful time, Uncle Dan."

"Good, good," he said absently.

Near the top of the steps, Julie said, "Tell me more about your new man, Uncle Dan. The one named Jed."

Serena's step faltered, then, stolidly, she continued to climb. Uncle Dan came out of his abstraction and his voice warmed as he spoke. He obviously liked Jed so much.

Serena tried not to listen. And, at the top of the steps, she paused then said goodnight abruptly, and left Julie deep in conversation with Uncle Dan.

She looked back once but they were still talking. Serena had hoped to ask Uncle Dan what had upset him for she knew he was still distressed. But she certainly didn't want to ask in front of Julie and Uncle Dan might not want anyone else to know what he had learned in the den.

Actually, she thought, as she opened her door, he might not want her to know. Castle Rock, after all, was his ranch. She had no claim. No right to interfere. She didn't want to interfere, she only wanted to help.

She gave one last glance down the hall, then shut her door. She would talk to Uncle Dan tomorrow. There would be plenty of time to talk to him tomorrow.

# Four

Serena moved restlessly in the wide double bed. Moonlight spread across her floor. She knew it must be late and the moon high. It was almost as bright as day. She closed her eyes firmly, but it didn't do any good. She just couldn't sleep. Images moved in her mind, Julie and Jed together, Will swaying on his feet, Uncle Dan's tired face in that last glimpse as she turned up the hall.

Sighing, Serena opened her eyes and looked at her moonlight-dappled room. It was such a lovely room, wide and deep, with sharply bright Indian art on the creamy adobe walls. The moonlight touched too her magnificent collection of Kachina dolls. Feathered headdresses glinted gold or green or red. Each Kachina doll, and she owned sixty-four, faithfully represented a Hopi deity. As a child, she had looked forward so eagerly to the times when the Pueblos permitted visitors to come and watch the dances. Each dancer's mask represented a god. Serena would eagerly match in her mind the huge swaying masks with her Kachina dolls. She knew them by heart, the Warrior God, the Corn God, the Snake God, the Rain God and so many more. It was Joe Walkingstick who had patiently taught her the story of each doll, making them figures of glory and power.

Serena smiled in the darkness. Dear Joe. She wished suddenly that she had talked to Joe about Jed. He wouldn't say much. That was not the Indian way. But whatever he said would be trenchant. She remembered his quiet observation last summer about Peter. "Not a man to hunt with." At the time, she had been shocked. That was before Julie took him away. Later Serena would remember and know that Joe had seen more than she. Because he was right. You couldn't trust Peter.

Serena bunched the pillow behind her head and wondered if Joe had ever said anything about Peter to Julie. If he had, it obviously hadn't mattered. But somehow, Serena doubted that Julie would have listened.

Julie.

It couldn't be like last summer. After all, Julie was married now.

That might not stop her. Julie was capable of going after Jed just because he was a handsome man and because Serena liked him. Julie would know that, of course. It probably hadn't taken her a day to sense that Serena cared.

Was that her motive? Was it spite?

But why? Why should Julie want to hurt her? Perhaps she didn't. Perhaps it was more instinctive than that, the automatic response of a beautiful woman to an attractive man without any thought at all of Serena. Or Peter.

Serena turned on her side and stared toward the windows. Then, determinedly, she shut her eyes and pictured Missionary Lake, high in the mountains, the deep soft dark water and moonlight rippling over it, and, finally, she slept.

When she opened her eyes again, the ghostly light of dawn touched her room with silver and gray. So, she thought muzzily, she had finally slept. It must be very early, not even five yet.

Far away she heard a door slam.

Serena sat up and strained to see the luminous dials of the clock on her bedside table. Who was up this early?

Gravel crunched beneath her window.

Serena threw back her covers and hurried to look out.

Uncle Dan walked swiftly down the path which led to the stables. He was carrying a rifle.

Serena frowned. Where could he be going so early and with a rifle? Then she shrugged. They were going to fly into Albuquerque about ten to pick up some medicine for one of the mares who had developed an eye infection. She would ask him then.

Suddenly dull with sleep, she turned back to bed and slept heavily until the alarm rang. She plunged into her morning chores and didn't have time to think about Uncle Dan or worry about Jed and Julie.

She was in the tack room just before nine o'clock when she heard the shouts. She knew immediately that something was wrong. By the time she reached the corral, a crowd was gathering.

Then she saw Senator. A boot hung from his left stirrup.

Joe was walking slowly toward Senator, a hand out-stretched. The horse sidestepped and his eyes rolled un-easily.

Jed was waving back the hands, making them give Joe plenty of room. "Senator's scared," he said quietly. "And he's dangerous. Everybody be quiet."

"Uncle Dan!" Serena cried out.

Jed turned and his face told the story. "Senator came back riderless."

"Oh my God."

The search began immediately. Three parties of riders set out in different directions.

"The plane," Serena said quickly. "Let's take it up."

She and Jed jumped into the jeep and drove furiously to the airstrip.

"I saw him leave this morning," Serena said bleakly as they took off.

Jed waited until the plane gained altitude. "Did you see which direction he went?"

"No. I saw him walking down to the corral." She peered out of her window at the dusty rugged country. "Oh, Jed, what do you suppose happened?"

He turned the plane to the west. "It's pretty obvious, isn't it? It's that damned horse. He rode him one time too many."

Serena didn't answer. Sure, Senator was dangerous. Everybody knew it but no one better than Uncle Dan. Uncle Dan knew how to handle Senator.

They searched in silence, each of them staring grimly down at the endless dun-coloured country and, coming closer now, huge reddish Castle Rock.

"Jed, look down there! Look!"

Jed slipped the plane down along the side of the immense rock, into the shadow that it threw, and there, like a crumpled sack, they saw him among the boulders. As Jed turned the plane, Serena pressed her hands against her face.

"Serena, I think I can set her down here. There's plenty of room and it's pretty level. Will you risk it?"

Her hands dropped. "Of course," she said quietly.

The Acrocommander hit hard, rose, hit again, then settled into a steady run. Jed eased her in a turn and they came alongside Castle Rock.

Uncle Dan's body was wedged between two big boulders.

Serena knelt by him, touched a cold hand, and tried not to see the bloody abrasions on his head and face. Jed stared silently for a moment. Then he began to walk along Castle Rock, looking down. After a bit "Serena, come look at this," he called out as he stopped.

When she joined him, she saw the glint of metal and then she remembered.

"It's Uncle Dan's rifle. He was carrying it this morning."

Jed frowned. "Are you sure? I've never seen him ride out with a rifle."

"He did this morning."

"I wonder why?" Jed asked slowly. He lifted his head to look up at the looming mesa. "Why would he bring a rifle here?"

"I don't know," Serena said uncertainly. "And why would he come here alone?"

They both looked at the desolate countryside, then Serena said quietly. "There's Uncle Dan's hat."

Jed went after it. He brought it back to her, the crown crushed, the brim smeared with blood.

"It looks pretty obvious," Jed said. "Mr. McIntire must have been dismounting—and Senator reared."

Serena could see it in her mind, the huge black horse, always so skittish, and Uncle Dan swinging his leg over Senator's back and then, just at that moment, something must have startled Senator, making him rear. Uncle Dan must have lost his balance, slipped, and then his boot heel hooked in the stirrup. Senator, spooky and dangerous and wild, must have started to run and the thing hanging at his side would have driven him crazy. Uncle Dan lost the rifle and then his hat and, soon, horribly soon, he would have been battered senseless.

Jed found a tarp in the plane and worked the body free. The two of them wrapped Uncle Dan in the tarp and struggled back to the plane and somehow Jed got their tragic load up and into the back.

The next two days were full of periods of frantic activity, and long slow agonizing hours of quiet. Father Dominguez came from Santa Fe to say the funeral mass. Ranchers came from hundreds of miles around. Serena directed Millie in preparing the huge meal to be served on trestle tables on the patio. She was so busy she had little time to realize her sorrow. But, as Father Dominguez said the final prayer and made the sign of the cross over the plain pine coffin, tears slipped down her cheeks.

The mourners stood in a semicircle, the family in front, around the edge of the grave which Joe and the men had dug the day before in the shade of a huge cottonwood near Blue Stone River, a half mile from the hacienda. Danny's face quivered and Serena slipped an arm around his thin shoulders and held him tightly. He was so little to lose his grandfather, to be left now with only Julie and Will as his family. Serena glanced at Julie. She wore a most becoming black dress. A black lace mantilla shadowed her face.

But Julie hadn't cried. Then Serena was shocked at her thought. That wasn't fair. Julie and Will loved Uncle Dan, too. After all, he had raised them just as he had Serena. The three of them and Danny were equally bereft.

Then, with a quiver of shock, Serena looked at Will. She had been so busy, trying to make sure the dinner preparations were complete and then helping greet Uncle Dan's friends from over the state, that she hadn't even thought of Will.

And now she must do something about Will.

Father Dominguez was stopping now to speak to each member of the family, clasping their hands for a moment. After he had spoken to her, Serena tried to move unobtrusively. She took Will's arm and pulled him along the path with her.

"Will," she whispered angrily, "how could you?"

He paused. His big body wavered ever so slightly. Quickly, Serena gave another firm tug and they started walking again.

"Shouldn't have happened," Will said slowly, thickly, each word an effort.

He was drunk as a lord, Serena thought angrily. Then she took a deep breath. It wouldn't help matters to be angry with Will. But what in the world was wrong with him? He had been drunk at the party the night before Uncle Dan died. Now he was drunk at the funeral.

Julie and Peter were leading most of the funeral party around the side of the house toward the patio. Even Jed was helping steer guests there. Jed had certainly managed to become Julie's second-in-command quickly.

But she didn't want to think of that. Not now. Not with Uncle Dan so newly buried. And she must see to Danny. She looked back for Danny then saw with relief that Joe Walkingstick was beside Danny, holding his hand. So she had time to try and do something about Will. It would be such a disgrace if Uncle Dan's friends realized he was drunk.

Once on the patio, she steered him toward a side door. He came along docilely until they reached the stairs. Then he tried to turn back.

"Got to talk," and he turned to go back through the den to the patio.

"Julie and Peter will see to everyone," she said soothingly. "You need to rest, Will. You can visit later."

He shook his head heavily. "Too late." He stared down at her and tears began to well in his eyes. "Too late."

"It is late," she said gently. "Time for you to rest, Will. Let me help you up to your room . . ."

"Don't understand," he said irritably. He licked his lips. His eyes opened and closed. For a panicked moment, Serena was afraid he was going to pass out. She must hurry, get Jed and Peter to help before any of the guests came into the house. Then, with a swell of relief, she saw Will open his eyes again and look at her blearily. "It's the sheriff," he said slowly and distinctly. "I need to talk to the sheriff."

He lowered his head and was about to start off again when Julie came up beside him. When he saw her, his big shoulders drooped.

Julie looked at him coldly. "Soused again?" Then she turned to Serena. "Come on, let's get him upstairs."

Serena hated it. She could see Will quailing before her eyes, but she too wanted to keep him from public view so she took one arm and Julie the other and they led him out. Upstairs, at the door to Will's room, Julie said, "I'll see to him now. Why don't you get back downstairs."

Serena returned to the patio and the afternoon passed as she spoke to all of Uncle Dan's friends, many of whom had come from far corners of the state. She thought of Will when Sheriff Coulter patted her shoulder. "Damn shame, Miss Mallory. We all thought the world of Dan."

"I know you did. And it means so much to us that so many of you came today."

The big man shook his head wearily. "I told him a thousand times to get rid of that horse, but Dan wouldn't listen. Damn shame."

Jed drew her aside once that afternoon. "Serena, I hate to bring this up just now, but Joe and I were wondering about the Hereford sale tomorrow in Roswell. Your uncle had planned to go and buy that bull from the Tomas ranch. Do you think we should go ahead?"

"I suppose so," she said slowly, "but perhaps you better check with Julie."

"Okay." He paused then asked gently, "Are you all right?"

Suddenly tears glistened in her eyes, but she said, "Oh yes. Jed, it's Danny we must think about."

"Joe's with him. He'll be all right."

A little later she saw Jed with Danny and it made the afternoon better.

Serena awoke early the next morning and lay sleepily, waiting to hear the clump of Uncle Dan's boots down the hall. Then, sickeningly, she remembered. She got up quickly and dressed and went down to the kitchen for breakfast and by eight o'clock was in Uncle Dan's office. She stopped for an instant beside the old red leather chair that had been his, gave it a light pat, then sat at her own smaller desk and reached for the ledger. She had plenty to do. She would bury her grief beneath mounds of figures.

When the door creaked open behind her later in the morning, she didn't even look up. She was deep in figuring the new price for baled hay.

"So here you are." The tone challenged.

Serena swung around and faced Julie. "Yes. Here I am."

Julie walked closer and looked down at the papers on Serena's desk. "What's all this?"

"It would be a little hard to explain all of it, Julie. I've been helping Uncle Dan with the ranch books and the correspondence since I came home."

Julie picked up the ledger, flipped through its pages, then dropped it back onto the desk. "I'll have Peter look it all over."

"Why?" Instinctively, Serena's voice was combative.

Julie raised an eyebrow. "Well, of course, the family will have to take care of things."

The family.

Implicitly, of course, Serena was not part of the family. That would be Julie and Will and Danny.

"I see," Serena said slowly.

"It's nice that you had something useful to do while you

were staying at the ranch, Serena, but now Peter and I can take care of everything."

Silence formed like a hard piece of ice.

Julie smiled sweetly. "And I did wonder what plans you were making?"

"Plans?" Serena's throat felt suddenly dry.

"Yes. Of course, with the secretarial training you have had, I'm sure you can get a job in Albuquerque. And we will be glad to give you a reference."

"A reference?"

"Of course. You can count on us. And we won't need your room until the end of the week. Then Peter has some business friends coming."

Serena pushed back her chair and turned and walked blindly out of the office. She could hear Julie's voice behind her but she wasn't listening any longer.

She had never, in her worst nightmares, imagined being banished from Castle Rock. Now it was happening and she was powerless to do anything about it. She walked heavily up the stairs and down the hall to her room. But, as she closed the door behind her, she realized with shock and despair that it wasn't her room at all.

# Five

The first pink rosy flush of dawn stained the eastern sky. Serena walked slowly down the gravel path to the stables. She went into the tack room, turning on the light. Saddles and bridles hung along the back wall. Her saddle was at the far end. She walked to it and reached up and touched the pale tan leather. Uncle Dan had given it to her on her sixteenth birthday to replace the saddle she had racketed about on as a little girl.

It was a beautiful saddle, handtooled with silver decorations, sturdy yet feminine.

She would have no use for a saddle in Santa Fe. She wouldn't have a horse.

There were riding academies.

Who would take care of Hurricane?

Hurricane was her horse. They had ridden together for eight years. Who would groom him? He loved carrots. Who would tuck one in hand then offer it when Hurricane nickered softly?

Stop it, Serena, she told herself. This is happening and you have to face it. It won't help to grieve over Hurricane. She would write Joe, ask him to look out for Hurricane, not give him to some hamhanded dude to ride.

When she had the money, she would send for Hurricane.

If, she thought bitterly, Julie would admit that he belonged to Serena. She didn't, after all, hold any bill of sale. Like the saddle, he was a gift from Uncle Dan. It had never occurred to Serena that she might someday have to prove that.

Damn it, Hurricane and the saddle were hers. So, room or not, foolish or not, Julie or not, she was at least going to take her saddle with her now. She reached up and swung it down.

Footsteps sounded outside the tack room. The door opened. "Hey, who's . . ." Jed stopped and looked at Serena in surprise.

It was the first time they had been alone together since they found Uncle Dan.

"You're certainly up early," Jed said finally. "What are you doing with your saddle?"

"I'm on my way to Santa Fe. And I'm taking my saddle with me." She said it bullishly, but, of course, Jed wouldn't try and stop her.

"Oh. Oh, yeah."

So he knew she was leaving the ranch. That meant Julie had told him. For the first time, she felt almost glad she was going.

"I didn't know you were leaving today."

"Yes."

He started to walk across the room toward her.

Serena swallowed and tried to keep on breathing evenly. It would never do for him to realize how he affected her. He was Julie's friend now. He reached out. "I'll carry the saddle for you."

His hand brushed hers.

"Thank you," she said breathlessly and she turned and hurried toward the door. He followed and they walked silently to the garage. He waited while she unlocked the trunk and he swung the saddle in.

"Where are your bags?"

"Up at the house."

"I'll carry them down for you."

"Oh, that's all right. I can manage."

"No, it's no trouble."

They talked politely, like strangers, but she wondered wildly if he felt at all the way she did. But no, she thought, confusedly, he can't or he wouldn't be Julie's conquest. So, only she felt that breathlessness and she must get away from him before she made a fool of herself.

"It will be a little while before I leave," she said brusquely. "I want to say goodbye to Hurricane."

He looked at her and she could see the compassion in his eyes. Sudden tears blinded her. Suddenly, she was in his arms, her head hard against his shoulder.

"Oh hell, Serena, I'm sorry."

Dear God, she thought, what's happened to me, to my pride?

She pulled away, turned her back to him. "It's all right," she said brightly, "really it is. I'm fine. And it's time I got out on my own. I've been thinking about it for a long time. And it will be fun to look for a job in Santa Fe." She wiped her eyes though trying not to look as though she had. "So thanks, Jed, but I'm fine. Now I'll go see Hurricane," and she started out of the garage.

"I'll come up and get your stuff in about half an hour," he called after her.

When she was in the cool, dark stables, her face pressed against Hurricane's mane, she felt like a fool, an absolute weak-kneed fool. How could she have flung herself at him? How embarrassing. Then her embarrassment faded, lost in her sorrow at leaving Hurricane. She patted him softly and rubbed behind his ears.

"I'll send for you," she told him. "I promise. I'll send for you."

Then it was time to go. She managed not to cry as she left the stables. She slowly walked back to the garage. The sun was up now, a shining orange on the horizon. She backed out her car and drove up the road toward the hacienda. The early morning sunlight touched the adobe with gold. She parked in the turnaround. The hacienda lay quiet as a sleeping lion. She had deliberately risen early so that she could leave before the ranch began to stir and waken. Even so, it was hard, so hard, to go. It would be impossible if everyone were there to say goodbye. She had told Joe and Millie last night. Their shock had been hard to bear. She didn't tell them Julie was forcing her to leave. Joe had spent most of his adult life at Castle Rock. The ranch was his life. She would do nothing to jeopardize that. If he knew Julie was forcing her to go, well, he might leave, too. It would be foolish but somehow she knew Joe didn't order his life doing only the smart thing.

And Joe must stay because of Danny.

So Serena closed her car door quietly and hurried back into the dawn-quiet house. In her room, what had been her room, she took one final look. A final look at the stately row of Kachina dolls, at the Navajo rugs, at Will's paintings on her walls.

This was goodbye. Goodbye to the happiest place of her life, to the only home she remembered. Goodbye to the kind of life she loved. Goodbye, even more finally and forever to Uncle Dan. Here at Castle Rock she could sense his presence, feel that he was near. Now she must leave and be alone.

Will burst into her room. A heavy flush suffused his face. "What the hell is this?"

Serena turned to face him. "I'm leaving Castle Rock, Will."

He looked down at the three suitcases. "Serena, you

can't." The anguish in his voice pulled at her emotions which were raw and strained.

Serena bit her lip. She would not cry. She would not. At least not until Castle Rock lay behind.

"Serena, why?"

"I don't . . ." She paused and swallowed. "I don't belong. I have no claim here just as Julie said."

Will reached out, grabbed her hand. "Julie. Did Julie say something to make you leave?"

"She made it clear that she and Peter would be running the ranch and that there wasn't any place for me."

"God damn," Will said heavily, furiously. "Why didn't you come to me?"

She squeezed his hand but made no answer. The stricken look in his eyes told her that he knew why she hadn't come to him. He had lain in his room the last two days since the funeral, the door closed.

"I didn't . . . if I'd . . . ."

Serena smiled determinedly. "It's all right, Will. I can't stay. Not the way Julie feels. I can't. So there isn't anything you could have done."

His face hardened. "Oh yes, I could have done something. I could have." Then he looked at her beseechingly. "Serry, do you hate me?"

"Oh Will, no. Never. You know that."

He stepped closer, reached out to touch her shoulders with his huge hands. "Serry, maybe we could both leave. We could start over somewhere. You and me."

She shook her head but her voice was gentle. "Too much has happened, Will. To both of us. This isn't the time to start something new."

"Yeah." He sighed. "Uncle . . . He was so damn good to us."

"I know, Will."

Somehow, it happened as naturally as water flows downstream, they moved into each other's arms and his head bent over hers. They held tightly to each other, each knowing the other's sorrow and seeking to console.

Then, Serena looked past Will and saw Jed standing in her doorway. For an instant, shock flickered on his face.

Serena pulled away from Will. Will looked around and scowled.

"I'll get your bags," Jed said impassively.

"Thank you," she replied, as remotely. Then she looked up at Will. "I must go now."

Will shook his head. "Serena, I'll talk to . . ."

"No," she said angrily.

Will sighed heavily. "All right, Serena. But I have to know where you will be."

Jed was picking up the two heaviest cases and walking toward the door.

Serena lifted up the smaller case. "I don't know where I'll be, Will. I don't have any idea."

He took the case from her. "Then call me as soon as you find a place. Serena, I have to know where you are."

"I'll call."

The three of them walked down the stairs and outside. When the luggage was packed, Serena slipped behind the wheel.

Will bent down, kissed her on the cheek, then, without another word, turned and walked away.

For a moment, Serena felt torn. She hated to see Will so unhappy. But she couldn't stay.

Then she and Jed looked at each other.

"Drive carefully."

"I will."

She turned on the motor. Just as she slipped the engine

into gear, Jed bent down and said harshly, "It's good you're getting out, Serena. Don't come back." Then he too swung on his heel and walked away.

Serena looked after him for a long moment then the Mustang spurted ahead.

Don't come back . . . don't come back . . . don't come back . . .

It rolled in her head like a refrain as the miles slipped away, the Mustang curving down mountains, down, ever down, toward Santa Fe. It was midmorning when she drove into town, passing the usual undistinguished buildings that sprout like weeds on the outskirts of towns all across America. Then she left the ticky-tacky buildings behind and was into Sante Fe proper with its narrow streets and low adobe houses and finally into the heart of the old city where Spanish musket fire and Indian arrows had struggled for supremacy.

It seemed familiar yet strange. She had been here so many times, to visit friends, to walk the narrow streets and look at paintings, but she had never come to stay. And she didn't know where to go.

She checked into a modest motel, bought a copy of the *New Mexican* and looked at the want ads. Three jobs looked promising. Before the afternoon was over, she had visited all three and her spirits were flagging. She didn't have enough experience or the job had already been taken or thanks for coming, we'll call you. She stopped at the park across from the Governor's Palace and rested on a bench. Across the street, beneath the portico, Indians sat cross-legged with their wares spread out before them on blankets. Tourists criss-crossed the park, stopping to photograph the Palace. It was all so everyday and ordinary—and Serena felt a tickle of panic at the back of her mind.

She had four hundred dollars in her bank account. That wasn't enough to rent a decent apartment in Santa Fe. It wasn't enough to buy food for a month. She had to have a job.

Grimly, she got up and started down a side street then a familiar name caught her eye. She stood outside the law offices of Williams and Honeycutt. She hesitated then opened the door and went in.

The receptionist smiled. "May I help you?"

"I don't have an appointment," Serena said hesitantly, "but I wondered if I could see Mr. Williams."

The woman looked at her inquiringly.

"I'm Serena Mallory. I used to live at Castle Rock, the McIntire ranch. But Uncle Dan, Mr. McIntire, was killed . . ."

The receptionist nodded, her face sympathetic. "Yes, of course. I'm so sorry. Mr. McIntire was a client of Mr. Williams for years." She flipped on the intercom. "Mr. Williams, there is a young lady here from Castle Rock, Serena Mallory. She would like to see you . . ."

"Send her in," the voice boomed over the intercom.

In an instant, Serena was walking into a book-lined office and a tall balding man rose from behind his desk to come around and take her hand.

"Miss Mallory, I'm so glad to meet you. Your uncle was one of my oldest friends besides being a client. I know how sad you are." His handshake was warm and vigorous. "Now, what can I do for you?"

Serena sat in a red leather chair and hesitated, but she had to ask. "Mr. Williams, Uncle Dan always handled everything for me and now—now I'm in a situation where I need money. If there is any."

Mr. Williams' face was suddenly very still.

"I mean, I'm not part of the family. I was just . . ."

"His ward. Of course, I know all about you."

So it wasn't going to be so hard, after all. Serena leaned back and relaxed. "Then you'll know what is left of my parents' estate. Uncle Dan always explained to me that the money he put into my checking account was from my parents. That's what I used for college and everything."

But Mr. Williams was shaking his head. "Actually, young lady, there was scarcely anything left when your folks died. I know because I helped clear up the estate. Your dad was just getting his start as a rancher and he was so much in debt that it took everything to satisfy the claimants."

"But the money Uncle Dan put into my account . . . ."

Mr. Williams smiled. "Dan McIntire was a generous man—and he loved you very much."

"I see," Serena said slowly. "I see."

So all those years, Uncle Dan had supported her as a member of his family. Serena thought of her college years, of the trip to Europe after graduation, of the sense of freedom and independence it had given her to have her 'own' money. It had always been there, a bulwark against the future.

Now it was gone.

"Serena."

She looked up at Mr. Williams.

"I don't want to pry, but what prompts your concern about money?"

She managed a smile. "Not having any."

"Oh, but that's not the case. Certainly not so long as you stay at Castle Rock."

"What do you mean?" she asked sharply.

He hesitated, then said good-humouredly, "Just what I said. You certainly won't lack for funds so long as you stay at Castle Rock."

"But I can't stay," she said unhappily.

"Why not?" And now it was his voice which was sharp.

She spread her hands. "Julie told me to leave."

He frowned. "Why did she do that?"

"I don't really know," Serena said quietly. "She just came into the office yesterday, I was working on the books, and said I would have to go."

"Well, she can't do that." He paused. "Look, Serena, I called the ranch yesterday afternoon and asked that all of the family and you come to my office tomorrow for a meeting."

"No one told me."

"I'm telling you now. The meeting will be at four tomorrow afternoon and I will explain the provisions of Dan McIntire's will."

"I'm not part of the family," she said, a little unsteadily.

"No," he agreed, "but the will directly affects you too, my dear."

The next day, Serena's mood alternated between hope and despair. On the one hand, lawyers do not speak loosely. If Mr. Williams thought she could stay on the ranch, then perhaps she could. Then Serena would recall Julie's face and the words spoken almost casually, ". . . we won't need the room until the end of the week . . . ."

What could Serena do if Julie opposed her return to the ranch? Nothing, absolutely nothing. Then Serena's spirits would droop and she would once again look at the tiny print of the want ads and feel that now familiar flutter of panic. What kind of skills could she offer an employer? She could keep books. She understood the workings of a big ranch. She could ride a horse. Not much there to earn a job in the city.

The next day she checked out of the motel at noon. She almost felt it was an omen. If Mr. Williams were right, she wouldn't have to spend another night looking at the bare and colourless walls of a cheap motel room, hearing the faint but irritating murmur of the next-door TV, the rush of water in nearby baths.

She reached the law offices at five minutes to four. The receptionist recognized her and smiled. "They are in the conference room down the hall, Miss Mallory. Go right on in."

Serena saw Julie first, of course. She was wearing a kelly green blazer and a crisp white skirt. Her blonde hair hung softly, swirling onto her shoulders. For an instant, she and Serena stared at each other.

"Come in, Miss Mallory, we've been waiting for you," Mr. Williams boomed. "Take a seat here, my dear, and I'll give everyone a copy of the will."

He bustled around the room, handing everyone, even Peter, a blue-backed copy of the will, then he took his place at the head of the table.

Serena sat next to Danny. He turned and whispered excitedly, "Serena, I knew you weren't gone for good. That's what Julie said but I knew it wasn't true." But his blue eyes looked at her imploringly.

She smiled and gave him a quick hug. "I don't know, Danny. We'll see."

Mr. Williams slipped on his horn-rim glasses. "I called all of the interested parties together . . ."

Peter interrupted. "But Miss Mallory is not an heir."

Mr. Williams nodded. "That's right, Mr. Carey, but she is a legatee." He cleared his throat, "Now, as I started to explain, I wanted to present the main provisions of the will to all of you in person because this is a very complicated instrument. All of you will be able to study it at your leisure, but, for now, I'll just sum it up as simply as I can." He looked around the table and for the first time Serena noticed how intelligent and penetrating his eyes were. "To put it in a nutshell, Castle

Rock belongs to Danny. Mr. McIntire had made earlier provisions for his sister, Jessica, and she is barred from inheriting from his estate.

"The bulk of the estate, the ranch and its operating capital, are left in trust to Danny. He will inherit all of it outright at his twenty-first birthday. Until Danny comes of age, Miss Serena Mallory will administer the ranch. Miss Mallory will receive a minimum of two thousand dollars a month in salary and, further, ten percent of the ranch's profits every year."

"Wait a minute," Julie said angrily. "Wait a minute, Serena can't just take over the ranch."

Mr. Williams looked at her quizzically. "I'm afraid I don't understand, Mrs. Carey."

"She's nobody," Julie said viciously. "Nobody. She isn't part of the family. She's . . ."

"Oh, let me explain," the lawyer said smoothly. "It isn't a matter of taking over the ranch, Mrs. Carey. Not at all. This is the disposition Mr. McIntire wanted. He told me, as a matter of fact, that Miss Mallory knew more about the workings of the ranch than either you or your brother, Mr. Pritchard. For that reason, he named Miss Mallory to run the ranch until Danny comes of age. He felt that a monthly salary and a percentage of the ranch profits would be a fair recompense. And, of course, she would live at the ranch and therefore not have any living expenses."

The last was put in so smoothly but Serena knew that Mr. Williams was making it absolutely clear, down to the last decimal, that Serena had her place at Castle Rock.

"Hey, it's a wonderful plan," Will said eagerly. "It's a swell idea." He looked at Serena hopefully. "You're going to take it on, aren't you, Serry?"

They were all looking at her now, Mr. Williams, Julie, Peter, Will, and Danny.

Serena stared down at the conference table, at the broad glistening expanse of oak, and she could almost, in her mind, see Uncle Dan's face in the shining wood. Uncle Dan had loved her and cared for her for so many years and now he was asking her to take care of his adored grandson.

Serena lifted her head and said simply, "Of course I'll come back to Castle Rock."

# Six

It took every ounce of Serena's determination to walk into the hacienda that evening. She had every right to be there. Uncle Dan's will had made that clear. Still, she couldn't help dreading that initial moment.

What would Julie do?

The family and the dudes always gathered in the den before dinner. Serena slowly approached.

Tonight, Julie was smiling as she talked to one of the dudes. Julie wore blue, of course, a brilliant metallic blue. The pleated silk skirt flared out in a circle. She was talking to . . . Serena searched her mind. So much had happened that the dudes had receded in her mind and now, taking up life again at Castle Rock, she needed to bring them back into focus. Julie was talking to John Morris, the stocky professor. His co-author, George VanZandt, was deep in conversation with Jed. Serena noticed that both the men were sunburned. They must have taken some time off from their work.

Serena saw Jed with a flicker of surprise. He must be eating with the family and the dudes now. At Julie's invitation? It must be.

Will and Peter and Danny and the Minters completed the group this evening. The Minters stood by themselves, looking bored.

Julie half-turned and saw Serena. Still smiling, she moved forward, holding out her hand.

"Serena, honey, we're so glad you've changed your mind and come back home. Peter and I both are so thrilled."

Serena allowed Julie to take her hand. She even smiled in return. So that was to be the story, that Serena had left to seek a career then changed her mind. It made her look a little erratic. But that was all right. She was so happy to be home that she didn't care how they carried it off.

After dinner, George VanZandt came up to talk to her. "I hope, Miss Mallory, that you don't think John and I are too self-serving since we have continued our stay here even though you and the family have had such a tragic loss."

"No, not at all," she said quickly though she had been a little surprised. The Rhodes had insisted upon leaving after Uncle Dan's death and had agreed to come back to the ranch later in the summer. The ranch had cancelled all bookings for the remainder of the month and half-expected that all the guests would leave. The fact that the Minters stayed didn't surprise Serena. They were so deficient in manners that nothing they did would occasion too much comment. But she had been a little disappointed that those nice men, Mr. Morris and Mr. VanZandt, had made no effort to cut short their stay.

"We would have left," VanZandt said earnestly, "but we are faced with a deadline. We have made every effort to keep out of the way this last week."

Serena had been too grieved and too busy to notice, but she said quickly, "I know you did. We appreciate it. Really, now we will be back to normal or as close as we can come to it this summer."

Mr. VanZandt smiled. "Then you won't mind if John and I continue our task."

"No. That's fine."

He paused then asked diffidently, "Am I correct in understanding that you are taking over management of the ranch?"

It still came as a shock to see herself as head of Castle Rock. But it excited and pleased her, too. "Yes." She took a quick breath. "I only hope I can do it justice."

"Oh you will, Miss Mallory. I'm sure of it." He paused again, was almost ready to speak then seemed to change his mind. "Well," he said abruptly, "I wish you the best of luck."

Serena looked after him curiously when he walked away. For an instant, she had sensed tension and a hint of something more to come, something important, then it was over and he was walking away. Serena shook her head. She must be getting nervy. So much had happened. Surely there couldn't be anything that George VanZandt could say to her that would really matter. Then she forgot about it, pushed it to the recesses of her mind, because Jed was walking toward her and something in his face made it very hard for her to breathe.

As neatly and efficiently as bulldogging a calf, he edged her down the room and out the french windows onto the shadowy terrace. They walked deep into the darkness beneath the magnolia. The thick sweet smell of the magnolia blossom enveloped them.

"Serena," he said huskily, "I'm glad you came back."

Then she was in his arms and his mouth sought hers hungrily, eagerly, demandingly, and the moment stretched into a warm rushing flood of timelessness and there was nothing in the world but the two of them, pressed together, nothing but the roar of blood in her head and the surging heat of desire.

She didn't care then about the ranch or Julie or her uncertainties about Jed, who he was and why he had come and his relationship with Julie. It was all swept away in the glory of that moment and she wanted it to last forever.

Abruptly, the lights that speared into every corner of the patio blazed into brilliance.

Jed dropped his arms from around her and stepped back. Serena felt exposed and defenceless. She raised a hand to shade her eyes.

Julie stood in the french window looking down toward the magnolia.

"Jed, are you there?"

"Sure." And he started up the path. Serena hesitated, then, feeling like a fool, followed him.

Julie made a little pirouette and the silky blue skirt swirled seductively. "Why, I can't start dancing without my favourite cowboy."

"Dancing?" Serena asked, her voice stiff.

Julie looked past Jed, raised one perfect eyebrow. "Why, Serena, I didn't see you there. But, of course, we should dance. Uncle Dan wouldn't want us to go moping about, draped in black. You know that."

She did know that. Still, it seemed too soon and heartless. She almost said so but Julie was holding Jed's arm now, drawing him inside.

He went, without a backward glance.

A bright red flush came up in Serena's face. She stood for an instant in the french window. Jed and Julie were already dancing, her body moulded to his.

Serena began to walk quickly across the room, her head high. Peter reached out as she came near. "Good heavens, where are you marching off to in such a hurry?" Then he smiled, his old familiar oh-so-charming smile. He was so sure of himself and his appeal. For an instant, she was tempted to leave him standing there enjoying his charm all by himself. Instead, she paused then asked flatly, "Aren't you a little confused, Peter?"

"Confused?"

She tilted her head back at the dance floor. "That's your wife. Over there."

He shrugged. "Certainly. I know that. But after all, Serena, we don't have to be provincial, do we?"

So that was his theme. While Julie dallied with Jed, he would find his amusement with her. Well, that might be his plan but she wasn't having any.

"No," she said quietly, "we certainly don't have to be provincial."

He slipped an arm around her shoulders. "So we can have this dance and . . ."

Serena stepped away. "Actually, no, Peter. You see, I've promised this dance to Will," and she turned and held out her hand to Will, who had been leaning disconsolately against the mantel.

The happiness in Will's face hurt Serena as much as anything that had happened. Before the evening was over, she danced with all of the men, except Jed. He remained close to Julie, laughing at her softly murmured jokes, bending near not to miss a word. Serena drank a little too much and knew it. It wasn't until she was in her own room, leaning back against the closed door, that she murmured, "Damn, oh damn," and let the tears slip down unheeded.

The next morning, her head throbbed, but she was up early. Firmly, she dressed, forced down a quick and solitary breakfast, and walked through the silent first floor to Uncle Dan's office.

Now it was her office.

There was much to do. She worked furiously, sorting the letters which had come in during the past week. Some she replied to immediately. Some she put in a reply-when-possible stack. Then she lifted down last year's ledger. It would help to know what Uncle Dan had been doing this time last year. It would give her ideas of what she should be checking up on now. And, of course, she would talk to Joe Walkingstick. Joe. Not Jed.

But it was Jed who knocked on the office door about nine. He poked his head inside. "Mind if I come in?" His tone was relaxed and casual.

She smiled impersonally. "Of course not, Jed. I needed to talk to you, anyway. Have you and Joe made plans to round up the new calves?"

Jed leaned against the side of the desk. She could smell the freshness of his flannel shirt and the faint citrus scent of after-shave lotion. She stared determinedly down at the ledger.

"Yeah," he said easily. "Joe and I thought we'd take a half-dozen hands up to the Sangre meadow Thursday. Is it okay if I draw for provisions?"

"Yes. I think it's a good time."

"Okay. Also, I wanted to clear something with you. I talked to Julie last week and she gave me the go-ahead to attend the auction at Roswell. Joe and I went and bought a Hereford bull. We can call and cancel if you disapprove."

"Of course not," she said quickly. "A deal is a deal. Be-sides, you and Joe know what you are doing. Tell me about the bull."

"Oh, he's a king all right. No doubt about it." Jed pulled an auction catalogue out of his pocket and showed her the squib on Big Harry. "Hell, he'll be so good at stud we'll draw service from ranches all over the state."

"That sounds great."

He was getting ready to go when she asked him the ques-tion she had carried with her the last few days.

"Jed, the day I left, you told me it was a good thing I was going."

He looked down at her, his face suddenly impassive, the

easy camaraderie gone. Perhaps she should have backed off then. But she could be stubborn.

"Jed," she continued doggedly, "you warned me not to come back. Why did you say that?"

For a dreadful moment, she thought he wasn't going to answer her at all. Finally, gruffly, he said, "Forget it, Serena."

"No."

She said it simply, but with a grave finality.

"Serena . . ." He grimaced. "Just be careful. That's all." And he turned and was gone before she could say another word.

Be careful. That was a warning, too.

She sat for a long time, looking down at figures she didn't see, her mind whirling with thoughts and guesses and conjectures.

There was something wrong at Castle Rock. Jed's brusque warning was only another in a series of odd incidents, Will's drinking, Julie's attempt to get rid of her, the strange presence of the Minters. Nothing by itself was too alarming. Taken all together they didn't make up a picture or a pattern but there was something that had disturbed the rhythm of Castle Rock.

With Uncle Dan gone, Castle Rock and the people on it, especially Danny, were her responsibility. It was up to her to find out what was wrong and make it right.

Serena pushed back her chair. She felt stifled and oppressed in the closed office. She needed air and space and freedom. But freedom was no longer really hers, she thought, as she went by the kitchen to tell Millie where she was going.

"Will you be back for lunch, Serena?"

Serena hesitated.

"I'll pack you a lunch," Millie said quickly.

Serena smiled gratefully. "I'd like that, Millie."

Millie wrapped a fried chicken breast in foil, added a dill pickle, chips, crisp carrots and two oatmeal cookies. "It's good for you to get out for a while, Serena."

"Do you think it's all right if I miss lunch here, Millie?"

"Sure. I'll tell Julie. It won't do her any harm to help out."

When Serena and Hurricane cantered out of sight of the hacienda, she felt a sweep of joy at getting away.

Getting away. She had never felt that way before on Castle Rock. Why did she want to get away? Impatiently, she urged Hurricane to go faster.

As they climbed, the path plunged beneath huge pines. The spicy aromatic scent and deep cool shadows delighted Serena. The path forked at Lightning Ridge. To the left, it continued to climb, a rugged sharp ascent, leading ultimately to the Anasazi cliff dwellings. The path to the right angled up then down to Lynx Lake where trout glided in deep clear pools and the icy water tasted as sweet and sharp as champagne.

Sunlight dappled the ground. The high still air rang with a quail's call and the sharp squawk of a raven. Hurricane, warm and strong, moved restlessly beneath her. She reached down, gently ruffled his mane and he made a soft sound in his throat. Hurricane loved to step carefully on the stony shore of Lynx Lake and dip his muzzle into the icy water.

Serena smiled and turned to the path on the right. She hummed as Hurricane carefully managed a steep descent. This was Castle Rock, this communion with nature. Soon the lake water glittered through the trees. She dismounted at the east end of the lake. Hurricane dropped his head and began to drink.

Serena settled on a sun-splashed rock to enjoy her lunch. Then, full and content, she stretched out and stared at the pale blue sky arching over the lake and the slender spruce trees crowding down to water's edge. This was what Castle Rock should be, infinite peace and beauty. Not a voice or footstep marred the silence. No alien presence disturbed the woods. But even this perfect Eden could not still the stirrings in Serena's mind. Sighing, she sat up and curved her arms about her knees and looked sombrely out over the still blue water.

Something was wrong at Castle Rock and she couldn't rest until she knew where the serpent lay.

Perhaps, she thought hopefully, her unease grew out of some unimportant imbalance. If she could trace the source of her fear, it might prove to be nothing that mattered at all.

What had been wrong at Castle Rock this summer?

Will, of course.

But who knew what tortured fancies drove Will? Even so, even allowing for an artist's burdened mind, Will's behaviour had been extraordinary. There was his odd reaction when Uncle Dan mentioned the telephone calls from New York. Then Will's distress when he learned Julie and Peter were coming to Castle Rock. Will had always been close to Julie. Julie was the stronger of the two, making the decisions, but, if there had been any break between them, Serena didn't know about it. So it made Will's unhappiness at Julie's arrival even stranger.

Strangest of all, of course, was Will's drunkenness the night before Uncle Dan died. That didn't make any sense. If Will often drank too much, that would be one thing. But he didn't. Some new, overwhelming, almost catastrophic pressure must be pushing on Will.

All right. Her job was clear enough. She must talk to Will as soon as possible and try to discover whether his unhappiness was linked to her uncomfortable sense of something wrong at Castle Rock.

Serena took a loose rock, threw it high into the air, then watched it plummet into the lake with scarcely any splash or sound. That was as much effect as the summer visitors usually had on Castle Rock. But this summer, perhaps they contributed to her sense of unease.

Take the Minters. Howard and Lou Minter.

Serena smiled wryly. Nothing about them suited the rugged and dangerous land. She pictured Howard's fleshy face and wary darting eyes, Lou's voluptuous figure and pouting mouth. They hadn't ridden a horse since their arrival. They seemed to spend their mornings sleeping and their afternoons and evenings watching TV, although he occasionally hit balls from the golf tee. Why should they have paid the stiff price it took to visit Castle Rock? And, even if by some wild mistake, they came to vacation, surely it hadn't taken them long to realize how unsuitable it was for them. Why hadn't they left? And why did they stay on after Uncle Dan died? Surely not because they were having such a wonderful time.

Life is, of course, full of unreason and perhaps the Minters were only a finite example of this law.

Serena pushed up from her rocky boulder and stood for a moment to survey the entire purple-blue lake. She couldn't imagine the Minters up here. Now, that certainly didn't hold true for the other dudes, George VanZandt and John Morris, the co-authors of a physics text. Both of them looked as if they would be quite at home around a campfire or climbing a steep rock-face. Serena wasn't sure what made her so confident of it, but she was. The only puzzle about them was the fact that they stayed on after Uncle Dan's death—and the reason might be as simple as VanZandt said, they had a deadline. Funny, though, how tanned they were to have spent hours closeted in their cabin, working on their text. Perhaps that claim was an exaggeration. As sensitive men, they wouldn't want to dwell on good times out in the sun while the family mourned.

It would be interesting, Serena thought, to look in their cabin, see the evidence of their work.

As she walked slowly toward Hurricane, Serena forced herself to consider another anomaly at Castle Rock this summer.

Would it be fair to say that nothing had been the same since he came? Jed had arrived two months ago, standing at the hacienda door, a duffel bag over his shoulder, an apologetic smile on his face. Lost, he'd said. Car trouble. Funny how well he had fitted in, how soon he became a new hand. Jed kissed her then turned and followed Julie. Jed warned her not to return to Castle Rock and, when she did, told her to be careful.

If Jed was not what he seemed, then what was he?

She remembered, with vivid clarity, the feel of his mouth against hers, the wild and lovely rush of feeling.

Serena jumped down from the boulder. Hurricane waited for her. She gave one last longing look at the lake but she had found no peace today. She carried unease with her as a leper carries disease. Now she must go back down the mountain and, whatever the threat that waited, face it down.

# Seven

As Hurricane stepped carefully along a narrow ledge with a 30-foot fall beneath them, Serena thought of that last lovely day when she had ridden out with Uncle Dan and Jed to Castle Rock. She and Hurricane had thundered down the trail. That reckless dash made Jed notice her. And Uncle Dan had cautioned her, not knowing that he would ride to his death the next day.

Oh, Uncle Dan, she thought, if you were here you would know what to do.

There was no answer to her silent cry, just the click of Hurricane's hooves on the rocky trail, the rustle of rabbits or 'possums in the underbrush, the cheerful summer chatter of the birds.

Then, abruptly, Serena reined in Hurricane and sat, her face wrinkled in thought.

How could she have forgotten?

She had tried to figure who might be part of this summer's strangeness at Castle Rock and she had thought of everyone but Uncle Dan himself.

The night before he died, Uncle Dan was furious.

The next day, Uncle Dan died.

Her heart began to thud as though she had ridden a hard race.

The idea was monstrous, unbelievable, impossible.

Anything that the mind of man can conceive can happen.

Serena understood that, but this time she didn't want to accept it.

"No." She said it aloud, to herself and Hurricane.

But her mind wouldn't be deflected. Accidents can be caused. Accidents can be arranged. Uncle Dan rode out to Castle Rock. If, when he started to dismount, something had startled Senator at just the right instant, Uncle Dan was vulnerable. It could have been done. Easily. A sharp rock thrown at Senator's flank. A gun shot nearby into the air. And, once the horse bolted, Uncle Dan wouldn't have had a chance.

Dead, Dan McIntire couldn't do a thing to stop whatever had so infuriated him the night before, and, if there was one thing certain, he had intended to stop it.

Serena nudged Hurricane with her knee and he began to trot. They were nearing the point where this trail diverged from the one which led up to the Anasazi ruins. Serena urged Hurricane to go faster. She felt a compelling need to get back to the ranch as fast as possible. She must make an attempt to find out what had made Dan McIntire so angry his last night to live.

If she could find the man he had been talking to . . .

She had barely heard the other voice. It was lower, softer. A man's voice? Yes. She was almost sure of that. But it could have been anyone, a member of the family, a dude, a guest.

Or Jed, she thought unhappily. It could have been Jed. It could have been anyone at all.

Serena slowed Hurricane when they reached a narrow wooden bridge that spanned a stream. His hooves cropped hollowly on the wooden spans. The water beneath hissed and gurgled. And, somewhere ahead, she heard a rattle of falling stone. Someone must be coming down the Anasazi trail.

"Hello," she called out. She reined in and waited for an answering call.

None came.

Again, distinctly, unmistakably, she heard the click of a horse's hooves.

"Hello." She leaned forward in the saddle, listening.

The hiss of the water, the vague rustlings of the undergrowth, the sharp wail of a raven, all these she heard, and nothing more.

Pine trees crowded close to the trail here. A prickle of unease touched Serena, the first faint stirrings of fear.

"Hello there. Who's coming?"

Hurricane moved uneasily beneath her. Did he sense her fear? Serena patted his shoulder.

Now, listen though she might, she heard no sound of another horse, nothing but the rushing of the water and Hurricane's measured breaths and the rustlings among the pines.

If anyone had been coming, they too had stopped.

Abruptly, Serena flicked her reins and Hurricane started forward. The path here ran deep among the pines, they pressed toward her, their thick resiny scent almost suffocating.

When they reached the fork, where the other path angled up toward the ruins, Serena stopped again. She looked up the path. If she had heard another horse, if her ears hadn't tricked her, it must have been on this trail. Someone could have reached this point in the trail, heard her shout and within a few yards been able to move off the trail and into the pines.

She scanned the woods. A white-tail deer looked warily at her.

Twenty riders could be hidden among the pines and she would never be able to see them.

But why would anyone ignore her call and plunge off the trail to hide?

The answer was obvious, of course. The rider didn't want to be seen, was determined not to be seen.

Serena sat stiffly in her saddle. Were eyes watching her at this very moment? Waiting for her to go?

Her face set and grim, she turned Hurricane down the trail back to the hacienda.

All right, she thought, all right. Something was very wrong indeed at Castle Rock but she wasn't going to be intimidated or fooled or deflected. She was going to get to the bottom of it.

The trail led past Will's studio. She would start with him.

Serena had always enjoyed coming to Will's studio. The entire southern exposure was a plate glass window. More light streamed in from two skylights. The studio always seemed to hold the gold of the sun within it.

Today the sunlight glistened as it always did but Will wasn't painting. He sat slumped in a leather chair, a brush loose in his hand, staring at a canvas on an easel. When she opened the door, his big head moved slowly, then, when he saw her, his face brightened.

"Serena, come right in." He started to move a stack of canvases from another chair.

"That's all right, Will. I can't stay long."

"Oh." He stood straight. "It's been a long time since you've come to my studio."

"I know." She looked away from his eager face and walked to the easel.

It was Castle Rock, of course, the huge mound of red rock with its thousands of fantastic shapes, but, instead of sandstone glistening in the bright sunlight, this immense rock was dark, bleached of colour, a sombre twisted tortured fretwork of pinnacles and caves, under a dark and foreboding sky.

Serena's breath caught in her throat. She whirled to look at Will. "Oh Will, you think so too, don't you? You think Uncle Dan was killed."

"No." He almost shouted it. "No."

She looked back at the painting. Unwillingly, his eyes followed hers.

"No." His voice was empty, now, dry as winter leaves. "No, Serena, I just painted it that way because that's where he died."

He wouldn't look at her. He began to fumble with his paints. Serena moved around until they were again face to face.

"Will, did you talk to Uncle Dan the night before he died?"

"Oh no." This answer came easily, with no hesitation and she could hear the relief in his voice. Then, wearily, he said, "Don't you remember, Serena, I was blotto that night." He jammed his brush into a water jar. "Dammit, I wish I had talked to him. I wish I had."

The sadness in his voice, the genuine sorrow, was more convincing than any denial. So it hadn't been Will in the office with Uncle Dan.

"Will," and she asked gently, "why did you get drunk that night?"

He still avoided her eyes, picking up a rag to dry the brush. He shrugged. "How should I know, Serena? I mean, you don't set out to get drunk. It just happens."

"Will, I've known you for a long time." She waited and finally, reluctantly, he met her gaze. "I know you, Will."

"Do you? Can anyone ever really know someone else?"

"Yes. You aren't a drinker, Will. So there must be something terribly wrong."

His blue eyes turned toward the window. He stared out at the undulating brown country with its delicate shadings from burnt sienna to russet to gold. "Sure," he said abruptly, "there's something terribly wrong. Sometimes when I start drinking, I can't stop." He looked back at her, his face drawn. "You didn't know until now. So I'm sorry, Serena. Damn sorry."

But again his eyes wouldn't meet hers—and she didn't believe him.

"Will, won't you tell me?"

"There isn't anything to tell," he said harshly.

"Will, I can't believe you could have had anything to do with . . . hurting Uncle Dan . . ."

That did jolt him. "Oh God no, Serena. No. I couldn't . . ." He didn't finished. "Serena, that's insane. Nobody killed Uncle Dan. It was Senator. You know Senator's a bad horse."

"If someone startled Senator when Uncle Dan was dismounting . . ."

She saw the horror in his eyes—and she could almost swear he had thought of it himself. But he shook his head. "No," he said violently, "no, it can't be." Then he looked at Serena broodingly. "Why do you think so, Serena? You have to tell me."

She didn't know how to put it into words, it was all so vague and formless. "I don't know if I can explain it, Will, but something's been wrong here this summer at Castle Rock."

"Wrong?"

"Just wrong," she said determinedly. "And that last night, Uncle Dan was furious."

That caught his attention, all right. Serena told him of the scrap of conversation she had overheard.

"Don't you see? Something bad was happening on the

85

ranch and Uncle Dan was determined to put a stop to it. And the next day he is killed—in an accident."

Will shook his head back and forth. "It can't be that," he said violently.

Serena couldn't understand why the idea upset him so much. Was it because the idea of someone having engineered Uncle Dan's accident was so repellent he just couldn't face it? Whatever the reason, she didn't want to devil Will any longer.

"You're just imagining things, Serena, don't you see?"

"Oh, I suppose so, Will. It's just been so awful, but I guess you're right."

"It's having to stay here," he said jerkily, "being trapped."

She looked at him in surprise.

"If we could get away . . ." He looked imploringly at Serena, "Serry, why don't we get married? You and I. We could live in Santa Fe. I could set up a gallery. We could find a house, a low adobe house . . ."

"But Will, why should we want to leave Castle Rock?"

"If we could be together . . ."

"Oh Will, no, we can't."

"Serry, there isn't anybody else for you so why . . . you and I, we've known each other so long. I've loved you for so long."

He held her shoulders, his big hands so gentle.

Serena could feel tears welling in her eyes. He was handsome and she had loved him for so long as a part of her life, a good part. But not the way she should love a man to marry him.

"Oh Will, you're so good to me. But I can't leave Castle Rock. I have to take care of Danny. And the ranch."

Will's face darkened. His hands dropped away from her. He turned and slammed a hand against a bookcase. "Damn Castle Rock," he said bitterly.

That was the picture she carried with her back to the hacienda, Will's face dark with anger and behind him the easel with that tortured painting.

It cast a spell over the rest of her day. Dinner seemed odd, too, Will taciturn, Peter aloof, Julie nervous, the Minters bored and the two professors politely talkative. The conversation ranged from a discussion of Minoan art to futures trading and Serena had trouble keeping any of it in mind. Directly after dinner, she excused herself, saying she had work to do in the office.

But when she reached the office, Serena didn't sit at her desk. Instead, she stood by the window that opened out onto the patio. It was raised about six inches. It must have been open like that the night before Uncle Dan died and she heard his angry voice so clearly on the patio.

Will denied having talked to Uncle Dan.

It could have been Will, of course. It could have been anybody . . . But why would one of the men on the ranch, either the family or one of the dudes or Jed, talk to Uncle Dan about something important during the party? Didn't it make more sense to guess that the other man spoke then because that was his only chance to see Uncle Dan? In other words, the other man must have been a guest.

Serena whirled around, walked determinedly to her desk. She called Luis Montoya at Crazy Horse Ranch first. He was friendly and polite but said he had only visited casually with Dan McIntire that night. Serena received the same response from Sam Berry at Dutchman's Creek. Then she called Bob Mackenzie at Burnt Hill. She had it down to an easy patter now.

"Bob, I'm sorry to bother you but I'm trying to get things in order here at Castle Rock since Uncle Dan died. And I wondered if you happened to be the man who talked to him in his office the night before he died?"

Bob Mackenzie didn't say a word.

Serena could hear the faint static and cracklings that always formed a background to ranch calls. She could picture Bob in her mind, tall, thin, with thinning red hair and tired green eyes. He never looked like he felt very good but he still rodeod and he was almost fifty.

"Bob?"

"I'm here, Serena. I'm thinking."

She felt a quiver of excitement. She was close. So close.

"So it was you."

"Maybe."

"Will you tell me what you said that upset him so?"

"Look, Serena, I'm not looking for any trouble."

"Neither am I. But I think I have some."

"What do you mean?"

"Bob, something odd is going on at Castle Rock. I don't know what it is. But I'm going to find out. And I think your talk with Uncle Dan could be part of it."

"Yeah," he agreed slowly. "It could be. It sure could be. 'Cause it's damned strange."

Then he told her. One of his hands, Luke Short, had been chasing some Burnt Hill cattle that had crossed over into Castle Rock land. Then he lost the steer, an old and canny one, in a thicket of pines. On his way back to Burnt Hill land, Luke passed Castle Rock.

"Yeah, Luke was just ambling along, in no hurry, and he said you could have knocked him over with a feather when he saw a plane taking off from that flat stretch of land like it was La Guardia or something."

Lots of ranches fly their own small planes. "It wasn't Castle Rock's plane?"

"Not unless you folks have started flying World War II

cargo planes. Luke said it was a C-9."

"My God."

"Yeah. And Serena, nobody's out for a Sunday hop in that kind of plane."

"No." She hesitated, then asked, "I don't suppose Luke could have been . . . mistaken?"

"Or drunk or crazy?" Bob Mackenzie asked drily. "No. Luke's solid. No bull from him. If he said he saw a cargo plane, he saw a cargo plane."

"What did he do?"

"Luke's not stupid either. He told me he slid away from there like a doe in game season."

Because it might not be a healthy thing to see a cargo plane take off from a desert. Serena understood that.

"When did this happen?"

"About a month ago. Luke didn't tell me until last week. He thinks things over. I thought about it and decided to tell Dan."

"And he was very angry . . ."

"Yeah. It about made him wild to think that kind of thing might be going on at Castle Rock."

Serena didn't have to ask him what kind of thing he meant. Planes usually landed at out-of-the-way places in Arizona and New Mexico for one reason only, smuggling.

"He said he sure as hell wasn't going to have anybody running dope on his ranch," Mackenzie continued.

No, Uncle Dan would have put a stop to it, no matter who was involved.

"Bob, I appreciate your telling me."

"Sure, Serena." He cleared his throat then, unhappily. "Hell, now I'm sorry I told Dan, messed up his last night. He always enjoyed the parties so much. If I'd had any idea . . . but nobody can know when an accident's going to happen."

"Oh Bob, don't feel that way. Not for a minute. You did the right thing to tell him."

After she hung up the receiver, Serena sat very still. If she had overheard Uncle Dan that night so could someone else.

The next morning he rode to his death.

But, as Bob Mackenzie, had said, no one can know when an accident is going to happen.

If it's an accident.

# Eight

"Serena, you look like you've seen a ghost."

"Do I, Julie?" Serena crossed to the bar. As she plopped ice into a glass, Julie persisted. "No kidding. You're white as a sheet."

Serena poured gin into glass then the Collins mix. As she stirred, she made a decision. "While I was in the office, I called some of the people who were at our party last week."

Julie took a handful of peanuts. "Why did you do that? Or may I ask? I know you are in charge but I suppose I can still ask questions."

"You may ask any question you wish at any time," Serena said carefully. "And I don't consider myself in charge. I'm just going to try and run the ranch the way Uncle Dan would have wanted it run, until Danny is old enough to take over. And that's why I was calling. I wanted to find out why Uncle Dan was so furious the night before he died and whether it had anything to do with the ranch." She said the last sentence loudly and clearly.

For an instant, it was absolutely quiet in the room.

Julie, of course, took it up. "Furious? Why he was no such thing! He had a wonderful time."

"Oh yes, he was furious," Serena said steadily. "I told Will I overheard Uncle Dan and that he was angry."

"I told her there was nothing to it," Will said loudly.

Serena faced his dark look. "But there was something to it,

91

Will. And now I know what it was."

She told them then of the ranch-hand and what he saw.

In the silence that followed, Serena tried to look at all of them. Will wouldn't meet her eyes. Peter looked indifferent, the two professors curious, the Minters bored, Julie excited. But it was Jed's face that made her chest ache. Jed looked simply furious and then, abruptly, his face was completely impassive.

Finally, Julie shrugged. "Even if a plane did land, I don't see what all the fuss is about. Or why it should throw Uncle Dan into a pet."

"Don't you, Julie?" Serena asked quietly. Then she looked at Howard Minter. "What do you think, Mr. Minter?"

"About what?" he asked truculently.

"About a big plane landing at an isolated spot on a ranch."

"I don't think a damn thing about it," Minter replied coldly.

John Morris' curious green eyes darted from face to face. "Well, it certainly has obvious possibilities."

No one else spoke and Morris continued a little uncomfortably, "It's the kind of thing you read about; smugglers landing out in empty country, unloading their stuff and taking off again. Is that what you're afraid of, Serena?"

Serena didn't have a chance to answer.

"Smugglers," Julie said excitedly. "My God, I leave this dust trap and the only interesting thing in years happens." Then her lovely face fell. "But it's all over with. I mean, here you are, Serena, all upset, but if it happened a month ago, it's all over. So what's the point in worrying about it?" She turned away and picked up a tape. "Listen, let's all dance. Make some excitement of our own."

The music blared on.

Serena turned to walk to the door. Jed caught up with her,

grabbed her hand and almost yanked her onto the dance floor.

"That was pretty damn dumb," he whispered savagely.

She looked up at his taut angry face. "Was it?" she asked defiantly.

They danced for a moment in angry silence, their bodies tense.

"Look, Serena, if . . . Godalmighty, if any of that's true, you've kicked a hornet's nest."

"That's all right. Maybe if they had any more flights in mind, they will cancel them."

"Jesus," he said quietly, "you are a dumb lady. Those kind of people don't get scared off by someone shaking a finger and saying, 'Naughty, naughty.' "

Now she was mad. So she was dumb, was she? "That isn't all I intend to do."

"What else? Write a letter to the editor?"

"I'm going to . . ." Then she broke off. Whatever she did plan to do, she couldn't share it with Jed. Who had been here a month ago? Who was a mysterious stranger come to the ranch with a ready smile and an unlikely story to explain his arrival?

Yet, she hungered for his touch, welcomed even this casual almost hostile embrace on the dance floor. How could she feel this way, how could she?

"Serena." His voice was soft now, caressed her.

Unwillingly, she looked up at him. His face wasn't hard and grim now. Instead, he looked weary. "Serena, I'm sorry. It's not any of my business. I'm sorry."

That's all he said, little enough, but she ignored the fears in her mind, shut them away, and relaxed against him. With a quiver of excitement, she felt his arms tighten around her.

"I didn't mean to hurt you," he said in a soft whisper

against her ear, his breath a gentle warmth. "God knows that's the last thing I want to do. It's just . . . well, it seems to me it's better not to say that kind of thing out loud. Don't you see what you've done?"

"What, Jed?" But she asked dreamily, not really caring, lost in the pleasure of his nearness.

"You've set yourself up as a threat to this smuggler—if there is one."

If.

"Oh, I think there is one," she replied slowly, the happiness draining out of her voice.

Jed made no answer.

She pulled back a little to look into his eyes. "Don't you think there is a smuggler?"

She couldn't read his face now, but she didn't miss the odd tone in his voice. "I would think," he said slowly, "that the odds are very good."

"What do you think I should do?"

"If I were you," he said emphatically, "I wouldn't do a damn thing."

"Jed!" She couldn't hide the shock in her voice.

"Shh," he said quickly.

Serena looked around but no one was paying any particular attention to them, except, perhaps, for Julie, whose vivid violet eyes slid by Serena's blankly. Too blankly.

Serena spoke more softly. "What do you mean?"

"I mean it's too damn dangerous. The kind of people who pilot cargo planes loaded with Colombian pot and Turkish cocaine are not going to roll over and play dead just because you warn them off."

"In other words," she said levelly, and her heart ached, "you want me to drop it, to look the other way, to let them use Castle Rock as a way station—and get away with it?"

"Yes." He grimaced. "Serena, do you know how much a pound of coke is worth on the street?"

She shook her head.

"About $34,000. A plane can easily carry $16 millions' worth." He said it slowly, lingering on each word. Then he asked grimly, "Do you know what some people will do for that kind of money?"

"Yes."

They danced without speaking, and Serena thought of Dan McIntire riding Senator out to Castle Rock—and not coming home again.

Was that what Jed was trying to tell her? That someone might try to kill her if she interrupted the smuggling? Was he warning her off? It certainly looked that way.

"Leave it alone, Serena."

"Is that what you want me to do?"

"Yes."

She didn't answer. She couldn't. There wasn't any way she could turn her back on it, pretend none of it had happened. She owed that to Uncle Dan. So she looked up at Jed and tried to smile. "Let's not talk about it now. Do you mind?"

"No," he said quickly, "I don't mind. There are a lot more interesting things I'd rather talk to you about."

"Such as?"

"You. And me. And the incredible luck that led me here to meet you."

"Luck?"

"Luck. Fate. Whatever you call it. Because there's only one of you, Serena. Only one. And if I hadn't come to Castle Rock, I'd never have known you—and my life would always have been incomplete and I'd never have known why."

Lovely words, magical words, words to thrill her heart,

bringing a glow and glory to the night. But, and the small still voice within couldn't be denied, were they words calculated to draw her away from the hard truth that his presence at Castle Rock wasn't a matter of luck at all?

She wanted to believe in Jed. If not forever, at least for this moment so she moved closer to him and said softly, "Tell me about yourself, Jed. All about you."

He didn't answer for a moment, but, when he did, his voice was amused, relaxed. "Autobiography hour? All right. But my life's been painfully dull until now."

The music was ending. They stopped near the french windows.

"Let's go outside, Serena."

On the patio, they walked arm-in-arm and it seemed so natural and right.

"The saga of a cowboy," he began in a teasing voice. "Actually, I grew up on a truck farm outside of Austin, Texas. I did have a pony and I worked part-time after school and on weekends and I bought a horse when I was fourteen. I always wanted to be able to live on a ranch like this—but I never thought I would."

And, despite herself, Serena began to figure how many pounds of cocaine it would take to buy a ranch like Castle Rock. She pushed the thought away.

"You seem to know a lot about ranches," she said quickly.

"I've worked on a bunch, especially summers while I was in college."

"Where did you go to school?"

Did he hesitate? Or did she imagine it?

"University of Texas. I majored in business. Accounting. My dad insisted. I hated it."

"You're not an accountant," she observed mildly.

He threw back his head and laughed. "Nope. I'm not. I've

never even tried it. I guess I really would have been a pretty good old-time cowboy, you know, signing up for a round-up, then moving on when the cows were in. I was in the Air Force for a couple of years. That's when I learned how to fly. Then I worked for a charter air service in . . . . oh, all over South America, mostly for oil or mining companies."

He had almost named a country. Would it have been Colombia?

"What brought you back to the States?"

And there was a distinct pause. A long moment of silence. When he spoke, the happiness was gone from his voice. "I came back because my brother was killed. I thought I ought to come home for awhile." He paused again, then said very quickly, "Then I decided not to go back down south. I was tired of it. I felt that something was missing in my life." Then his voice dropped and he pulled Serena close to him, "And now I know what it was. Oh Serena, you are so beautiful."

Happiness poured over Serena like sunlight flooding a plain. It was not until later, as she walked slowly upstairs, the warmth of Jed's embrace a memory, that the cold niggling hateful thought came that Jed certainly had managed to distract her from asking any more about him. But she did have a fragment of fact, something concrete to trace. He had said he received a degree in accounting from the University of Texas. That should be easy enough to check.

The next morning, when she was sure no one was near the office, she placed the call to Austin. She was transferred several times before she hooked up with the right office.

"Yes, I'm trying to fill out some records on a new employee and I need to know the year he received his degree. The name is Jed Shelton and he probably was graduated four or five years ago. He was from Austin and received a degree in accounting."

She waited patiently, idly doodling on a legal pad. The girl came back twice, checking to be sure she had the correct spelling and hometown, then finally she said, "I'm sorry, I can't seem to find it. No one named Jed Shelton from Austin was graduated within the past ten years."

Serena had trouble thanking the girl because it was suddenly so hard to breathe. After she hung up, Serena stared miserably at the legal pad and the row of plump-bellied planes she had drawn while waiting.

Jed was not what he seemed.

That simple sentence said it all. Broke her heart and said it all. Because, no matter how she felt about Jed, wanted to feel about him, she owed her loyalty to Danny and to Castle Rock.

Grimly, Serena ripped off the top page of the legal pad and began to write. In a few minutes, she studied her plan of attack. Then she got up and set out to tackle the first job.

She found Joe Walkingstick at the training corral, working in soft sand with a new horse.

Serena climbed up and sat on the top rail. Joe worked gently with the trembling horse, getting him used to the bridle. In a few minutes, he nodded in satisfaction then turned and walked over to Serena.

"Are we still going to have the Fourth of July rodeo, Serena?"

She looked startled. "Golly, Joe, I hadn't thought about it."

"We've done it for a lot of years."

Serena knew that was true. She couldn't, in fact, remember a Fourth when there hadn't been a Castle Rock Rodeo. It wasn't, of course, a big public rodeo. It was for family and friends with men from nearby ranches competing in bronco riding and bulldogging, the prizes mostly tack donated by Uncle Dan. It brought lots of guests with campers and tents. On the night of the Fourth, Castle Rock put on a huge barbecue and fireworks show.

"Can we get everything ready by then?"

"We have two weeks. I think we can do it. I went ahead and ordered the lumber to build the temporary grandstand by the main corral."

Serena thought suddenly of the clean sweet smell of new lumber. She and Will and Julie had loved the grandstand when they were little, so pleased at a giant toy.

"I'll need to order enough food. Will you see to slaughtering the cows?"

"Yes, of course. Millie's been planning for about 150. Don't you think that's about right, Serena?"

"I think so. Maybe we ought to have enough for 200. Don't you remember? Last year, so many of the ranchers brought guests."

They talked for a few minutes more, discussing the work that needed to be done in preparation, then, as Joe was turning to leave, Serena said, "Joe there's something important I need to talk to you about."

He listened quietly as she told him about the Burnt Hill cowboy's report of a plane taking from Castle Rock.

"A big plane?"

"Yes. And you know what that means."

Joe nodded. "It's happened on other ranches." He frowned. "Sometimes, it's the foreman who's involved. You aren't thinking . . ."

Serena reached out, touched his thin strong arm. "Oh Lord no, Joe. I know it's not you. I know that." And she did. Some things you know beyond any possibility of doubt.

"But it has to be somebody here on the ranch."

"I know."

"I'd swear by our men, Serena. I can't believe any of them could be involved in something like that."

"I know," she said again.

"Then that would mean . . ." Joe's voice trailed off. He didn't go on to say the obvious. If it had been someone on the ranch a month ago and you excluded the cowhands that left only Uncle Dan, Will and Jed.

Uncle Dan was dead. That left Will—or Jed.

It could be Will. Serena hated the way her heart lifted. But it could be Will. He had not been himself, all summer long. And it must have been before the plane came that he had all those long-distance calls to New York that made him so uncomfortable. If it were Will, he would have to have partners who would take the drugs and market them.

But Will hadn't lied about where he went to school. Will hadn't come to the ranch with a patently phony story.

"Serena." Joe spoke her name softly.

"Yes?"

"Maybe . . . maybe it would be better to let sleeping dogs lie?"

So Joe, too, feared where the trail would lead.

"But I don't think it's over, Joe."

"What can we do then?"

"We can watch for anything odd, anything out of the ordinary. And you can watch Castle Rock. There have to be some preparations before a plane could land. Maybe a landrover hidden among the rocks to carry out the crates. I want you to go by Castle Rock at least once a day, but don't tell anyone what you are doing. Will you promise me that?"

"Sure."

She reached out, clasped his hand for a moment, then she jumped to the ground, stood by him. "And Joe, that includes Jed."

He looked at her in surprise.

"It's just between you and me, Joe."

He nodded.

Serena left him looking after her as she walked quickly toward the stables. As she saddled Hurricane, she wondered if she should have told Joe more. But she didn't know anything for a certainty. It was all conjecture and every surmise hung from the tiniest of threads. Still, she had been right to warn him against Jed.

It wasn't until she and Hurricane were out of sight of the hacienda that she realized she had turned him toward Castle Rock.

Castle Rock glittered blood-red in the hard noon sunshine. Serena slowly circled the huge mass, not looking at the wind-and-rain carved cliff face, but at the cave mouths and tumbled boulders.

An army could hide here.

Even now someone could lie in the dark mouth of a cave and watch her circle and she would never know it.

Is that what happened to Uncle Dan? Someone in a jeep or on horseback could have arrived before him and waited in the shelter of the rock.

A shiver tingled her back.

It was a fancy, of course. She was all alone here in the noonday sun, she and Hurricane.

Then, patiently, she began to walk Hurricane, this time looking at the rock-strewn ground. She had gone only a hundred yards when she found it.

The huge rock-built X lay there unchanged from the day when she and Uncle Dan had ridden out with Jed to see it. That seemed a hundred years ago, that day when she had so lightheartedly and, admit it, daringly, ridden Hurricane down the mountain trail to try and impress Jed.

It was Jed who spotted the Xs from the Aerocommander and brought Uncle Dan and her to see them.

If Jed were a smuggler, waiting for a cargo plane to land at Castle Rock, would he show the ranch owner the two big Xs marking either end of an improvised runway? For surely that had to be the meaning of those carefully arranged rocks, to point the way to a pilot unfamiliar with his destination. Of course he wouldn't. For an instant, Serena felt a thrill of hope, then she sighed. It could be a kind of double bluff, the earnest new young cowhand showing ahead of time his lack of complicity should a landing be observed in the future.

"Oh hell." Serena said it aloud. She didn't know. No matter what she learned, she kept coming back to Jed's presence on the ranch when the Burnt Hill hand saw the plane taking off.

Serena looked back up at Castle Rock, at the honeycomb of caves and crevices.

Jed had been on the ranch. Jed and Will.

That's who it came down to.

Serena sighed. That made sense, lots of it, but it didn't explain her funny feelings about the Minters or the two professors. She could see the Minters as drug smugglers. They would think of it as a good business deal, never even considering the kind of evil it created.

But Howard Minter hadn't been at Castle Rock a month ago.

Serena flicked the reins and Hurricane began to move.

Still, he could be part of it, coming perhaps to oversee the arrival of a very big shipment. That could be. That could very well be, she thought with a surge of excitement. Minter might want to oversee the unloading in person, not trusting his conspirator on the ranch. Minter might want to make sure that absolutely all the drugs were being sent to him and not a tidy extra amount stashed away in the caves for the sole benefit of his partner. And the same kind of reasoning could apply to the professors, the professors who were so tanned and ruddy and who spent so little apparent time working on that famous physics text. They were charming men, kindly men, but the prospect of huge amounts of cash had been known to corrupt a great many charming people.

When she reached the jumbled mound of rocks where Uncle Dan's body had been wedged, Serena reined in Hurricane and stared down at the silent stones. Then she shivered. Uncle Dan had been in his own country, the world he knew and trusted. He'd started to dismount and, somehow, Serena was coldly certain of it, Senator had been startled, made to bolt.

It took a special viciousness, a terribly overweening callousness, to destroy another human being. Somewhere on the ranch, behind a smile she knew, a hand she had touched, this malignant being existed—and only she knew it.

# Nine

It wasn't going to be easy to search the Minters' cabin because Lou Minter spent most of the day lying on her bed, pillows fluffed behind her, watching TV and eating chocolates.

The next day Serena waited impatiently until midmorning then she walked down to the garage. She went into a supply shed, picked up a couple of fuses, a flashlight and a screwdriver. She took time to walk up beyond the stables and look out toward the driving range. Satisfied that Howard Minter and Peter were there, she turned and walked briskly to the Minters' cabin.

At her knock, a sulky voice called, "Come on in."

Serena stepped into dimness, the only light the flickering sheen of the TV screen.

"Mrs. Minter, I'm sorry to bother you but we're having some electrical problems and I need to check the fuse box in your closet."

Lou Minter looked disappointed. "Oh, I thought maybe you'd come to talk. I'm so sick of watching this stupid TV I could scream."

For a minute, Serena almost felt sorry for her. If ever someone had been thrown out of their own milieu into a strange and alien environment, it was Lou Minter. Serena felt at a loss because what could she offer? She was busy throughout the day, working in the office or out riding. Julie was . . . What was Julie doing with her days? Probably riding out with Peter or talking to Will. And that left only Will and the two professors. Ostensibly, the professors were busy. So, with a little pang of guilt, Serena offered up Will.

"Have you been to visit Will's studio?"

Lou flicked off the TV and sat up straighter against her pillows. Her sheer lacy nightgown gaped. "Will. That's the big redheaded guy?"

"Yes. He's a painter."

Lou tossed her head and her thick wavy blonde hair cascaded like molten gold. "Come on and sit down."

Serena hesitated then accepted the invitation.

"What's he paint?"

"Still-lifes mostly and country scenes, the mountains and the desert."

Lou grimaced. "Mountains and desert, you've got too much of both of them. God, I hate this place." Then she said quickly, obviously not wanting to lose her audience, "Hey, I don't mean to insult you. It's just . . . I'm not used to all this space," and she waved her hand.

Serena thought Lou wasn't being overwhelmed by space so long as she clung to this cluttered, closed room with its heavy scent of cigarette smoke and chocolates. She managed a smile, "Oh, I know how you feel, I think. A city crowds me, closes me in, so I suppose it's all in what you are used to."

"That's it exactly," Lou agreed.

"So you haven't spent much time in the country?" Serena probed gently.

"First time. Last time if I have anything to say about it."

"What prompted you to come to Castle Rock, feeling that way?"

Abruptly, a cautious careful look came over Lou's face. "Oh, we thought it would be fun, something different," she said carefully.

105

"Has it met your expectations?" Serena asked lightly.

At Lou's blank look, Serena said gently, "I mean, has it turned out to be what you expected?"

Lou shrugged. "I guess I didn't know what it would be like. I didn't know it would be so . . . so big."

Serena leaned back in her chair and smiled. "Where do you live in Los Angeles?"

"Brentwood." Uncharacteristically, Lou didn't add another word.

"What does Mr. Minter do?"

"Do?"

Serena decided to continue as gracelessly as she had begun. "What is his work?"

"His work? Oh, he owns things, runs businesses and things like that."

"That must be very interesting."

"Oh, sure."

"Do you help him?"

"Me?" Lou laughed and it was the first time Serena had detected genuine amusement. "Oh no, honey, I don't work. I just . . . help him play."

And that, Serena thought, is as far as I want to go into that. Briskly, she got up. "Well, I'd better check those fuses."

"The fuses. Oh, sure." Lou looked blankly around the room.

"I believe they are back here in one of the closets," Serena explained blandly as she walked across the room, trying to see as much as possible in the few seconds she had.

All the cabins were generally the same, a square good-sized room with two double beds, a fireplace, TV and several comfortable chairs. A little kitchenette was tucked in an alcove past the fireplace.

The room was cluttered, magazines spread over the coffee

table, an open suitcase propped on one chair with a mound of clothing peeping over the sides. Soiled dishes, some with the sticky residue of ice cream, sat next to overflowing ashtrays and empty drink glasses.

Nothing different from a thousand motel rooms.

Serena opened the closet door, chattering all the while. "Yes, I'm pretty sure the fuse boxes are tucked back here somewhere. I'll be careful among your things." Now she was out of Lou's view. Serena snapped on her flashlight, ran the beam over Lou's dresses, such totally unsuitable clothing for a ranch vacation, and among his suits. He did at least have slacks and polo shirts to wear. The flashlight beam stopped, wavered and held. Serena's heart thudded. The shiny leather of the holster glistened in the light, emphasizing the dark blue of the gun. Serena didn't have any idea what kind of firearm it was but she knew it was a handgun and it looked big and deadly. Then she dropped the beam to the floor and swept it back and forth. There, at the very back of the closet, just beneath the fuse box sat two walkie talkies. Serena stepped closer to them.

"Oh, Howard, I didn't know you were coming back this early. I'm not dressed yet."

"Yeah."

"Serena's fixing a fuse or something."

Serena heard his explosive, "What?" and the heavy sound of his footsteps. Quickly, she stepped forward, opened the fuse box and flipped the switch that controlled the outside lighting to OFF.

"Here's the problem . . ."

The door was yanked wide. She looked around. "Oh, Mr. Minter, how are you? You did startle me. But I've found the problem," and she reached up and flipped the switch to ON.

He looked at her, his heavy red face alert and suspicious.

Serena smiled. "Everything's fine now," and she closed the fuse box door and started out.

For a moment, he stood unmoving, blocking the way, looming over her, then, slowly, he stepped back.

"I'm afraid the wiring is pretty old," Serena said with a disarming smile. "We have lines hooked up to fuse boxes in the oddest places."

"Yeah," he said heavily with no answering smile.

She stopped at the door to thank them again, then plunged out into the bright sunshine, terribly grateful to be free of that dim closed room and him. She had had a moment of real fear when he blocked her exit from the closet. She didn't breathe easily until she was out of sight of the Minters' cabin.

Serena felt just as she had the day several years ago when she rode up to a spring and disturbed a brown bear with her cub. The mother bear had turned toward her with the same malevolence that she had seen in Minter's eyes. Wild beasts are dangerous, dangerous and deadly, and Serena knew it as well as any rancher. You do not disturb dangerous animals. If it happens, you move slowly and carefully and quietly.

She didn't know exactly what her visit to the Minters' cabin proved. It made clear only one thing in her mind, Howard Minter wasn't a man to trifle with. That didn't mean she could link him to smuggling or murder, but it made him a suspect.

Serena reached the point where the path diverged, the down trail leading back to the ranch, the up trail to Desperado Point, the professors' cabin.

She had checked on the Minters. Now was the time to check on the professors.

The ride up the cabin was so much a part of a perfect summer morning that it made her suspicions seem so incredible. But, when she knocked on the cabin door, there wasn't any answer. Those hardworking professors weren't in.

Fishing her keys out of her pocket, Serena opened the door. She took a last long careful look then stepped inside. After a moment's thought, she left the door open behind her. If they should return unexpectedly, she could always use her fuse story again.

This cabin sparkled with cleanliness. No clutter marred the tables. Each bed was made with military precision. Serena walked over to the wooden table in the kitchenette. This was the only surface which would be suitable for spreading out a manuscript. It was clean and bare. She walked quickly around the room. Nothing on top of the bookcases, nothing on the low coffee table.

Did they bundle up the manuscript, carry it with them on their daily rides? Or was the manuscript as imaginary as their professorships?

Sunlight slanted through the two east windows, spilling cheerfully on the clean bare emptiness of the room. Suddenly the very bareness seemed sinister to Serena.

Who were these men and why had they come to Castle Rock?

She whirled around and hurried to the closet.

She saw it at once, of course. The trunk absorbed most of the space in the narrow closet. There was nothing especially remarkable about the trunk except for the shiny new padlock through the hasps.

Serena stared at the padlocked trunk for a long time. It could, of course, hold the famous manuscript. It must certainly be a fantastic physics text to warrant so much security.

She gave the lock a yank, not expecting anything. It didn't budge.

The rest of the closet didn't do much to allay her suspicions. The Levis and work shirts she would expect, but several pairs of hiking boots lined the closet floor. Hiking boots make all kind of sense in rattlesnake country, but weren't these men here to closet themselves in their cabin to revise a manuscript? Why should they need a couple of pair of hiking boots apiece?

Serena knelt, picked up one boot, and brushed powdery gray dust from it. She knew that kind of dust, fine silty gray dust that hung smokily in caves and inches deep in tumble-down ruins. When disturbed, it stirred and flurried and clung.

Serena replaced the boot then rose and left the closet after one final look at the trunk. As she closed the cabin door behind her and remounted Hurricane, she tried to assess her discoveries but her mind was a whirl of conjecture.

After lunch, which the professors didn't attend, she settled down to work at repair jobs in the tack room. She was determined to be there when Morris and VanZandt returned.

Danny joined her about three.

She put down a halter she was working on. "Hi Danny. Are you going to take Buster out for a ride?"

Danny nodded. "In a little while." But he leaned against the workbench and made no move to get his saddle.

After a minute, Serena looked up. "Want me to help you saddle up?"

"No."

Dark smudges under his eyes emphasized the paleness of his face. He was so little, Serena thought, to be alone.

"Oh Danny," she said cheerfully, "I've been meaning to talk to you. Don't you think we should go ahead with the annual Fourth of July rodeo and barbecue?"

"Oh sure, Serena, sure. Hey, I'd forgotten about it." A faint flush of excitement touched his cheeks. "Hey, do you think Joe will let me ride Buster in the calf roping?"

"Gee, I don't know," she said slowly. She didn't want to discourage him but she felt sure he wasn't strong enough yet to try that event. "Is Buster really ready for it?"

"Oh, yeah. Yeah, Buster's great."

She was smiling by the time Danny finished. "Well, we'll see."

"Aw, Serena, I can do it."

Serena picked up another halter and reached for an awl. She knew Danny was watching her closely. She let him break the silence.

"Hey, Serena?"

"Yes."

"You won't go away again, will you?" There was, toward the end of his sentence, a very tiny tremor in his voice.

"Of course not," she said quickly, firmly. She looked directly in his eyes. "I promise you, Danny. I won't go away."

"They can't make you leave again?"

Surprise must have shown in her face.

"I know what happened," he said quickly. "I heard Julie telling you to go that morning."

"Oh." Serena didn't know what to say. She didn't want to drive a wedge between Danny and his cousin, but she couldn't lie about it.

He saved her the trouble of answering when he said angrily, "It's all Peter's fault."

Serena laid down the awl. "Danny, what makes you say that?"

He looked at her uncertainly. "Do you like Peter?"

Serena avoided his eyes. "Actually, Danny, I don't know Peter very well. I met him last summer when he came here as a dude. Then he and Julie fell in love and were married in the Fall."

"You hung around with him a lot last summer."

Childish eyes see so much.

Serena stared down at the halter, picked up the awl and began to turn it against the leather strap. "Yes, I suppose that's true. Still, I don't feel like I know him very well." And that, she thought, was a fair enough statement.

"He doesn't want you to stay at Castle Rock."

"How do you know that?" Serena asked sharply.

"I heard him tell Julie to get rid of you. It was the night before she told you to get out of your room."

Danny put it simply with a kind of brutal clarity. That was exactly what Julie had told her.

"So Peter wanted me gone?"

Danny nodded. "Yeah. He was talking to Julie under the magnolia tree. I was up pretty high and they didn't see me but I could hear them. He said . . ." Danny paused and then his voice took on a deeper crisp tone and Serena knew he was remembering Peter's very words, " 'we need to get rid of Serena. Then we can have the ranch to ourselves.' "

"I see."

"Serena, what about me?" Danny's voice was suddenly young and thin and vulnerable again. "What were they going to do with me?"

"Oh Danny, you don't need to worry. You don't ever need to worry. If I left, Julie and Peter would take care of you. The ranch belongs to you. You don't ever have to worry about your place at Castle Rock."

Danny's underlip jutted out. "I don't want to stay with Peter and Julie. I don't like Peter."

This wouldn't do. Julie was Danny's cousin and Peter was his cousin's husband. Serena managed a laugh. "Hey Danny, simmer down. You're borrowing trouble. Don't you remember how your Grandad always told us not to borrow trouble. Well, that's pretty good advice. Now, I can tell you've been sitting around with too much time to think and not enough good things to think about. And I'm up to my ears in work and need a deputy so you are going to be my man. Seriously, Danny," and she suddenly spoke as one adult to another, "I need your help with the Fourth rodeo. I want you to talk to Joe and tell him we need to bring in a bunch of wild horses. Why don't you organize that round-up and I'll get in to Santa Fe to see about the fireworks and the prizes."

After Danny left in high excitement to search for Joe Walkingstick, Serena stared thoughtfully out the door.

So Peter wanted her off the ranch. And, obviously, Julie did what Peter wanted. That shouldn't surprise her, but somehow it did.

Why should Peter and Julie want to stay at Castle Rock? All Julie talked about was Cannes and St. Moritz and Acapulco. And Peter had certainly never shown any great interest in the ranch. He did ride out fairly often, but he never asked about the herds or water or the outlook for beef prices.

It didn't make any sense.

Especially not the fact that Peter wanted Serena off the ranch. Why? Did he want to take over the management? But that would just be a lot of hard work and it wouldn't be possible to cheat Danny because the lawyer for the estate would keep a careful accounting of all monies. Besides, Peter and Julie apparently had a great deal of money because Peter didn't have to work.

Personal dislike? Somehow, Serena doubted it. She had never, she thought with grim honesty, affected Peter that powerfully, one way or the other.

But the fact that Peter was behind Julie's effort to rid the ranch of Serena seemed just another indication that nothing was normal at Castle Rock this summer.

Serena twisted the awl, making the final hole in the strap,

then she lifted her head and listened. Hurrying, she hung up the repaired bridle and went to the door of the tack room.

The two professors, hot, dusty and weary, were coming down the path, carrying their saddles. They smiled when they saw Serena. She smiled in return and held the door for them.

"It looks like you've had a hard ride."

"Hot out there this afternoon," Morris replied, his round face flushed and sweaty.

"Oh, did you ride out into the flats?"

Morris was swinging his saddle upon its hook. He paused and looked at VanZandt before answering and Serena knew what flashed through both their minds. It wouldn't be hot riding the trails up into the mountains but hardly anyone would pick a blazing afternoon to ride out into the scrub country.

"I suppose we're just out of shape," VanZandt interposed smoothly. "Actually, we usually go up toward Lynx Lake but it can take it out of old duffers like us."

They didn't look like old duffers. They looked fit, tanned and hardy.

"It's nice," Serena observed mildly, "that you are able to take time away from your book and get out to ride."

Morris looked at her sharply, but her face was bland and pleasant.

"I wish we could concentrate on the scenery," Morris responded, "but we are really just a mobile work room. We do revisions as we ride."

Serena just looked at him. She was, she thought irritably, not that damned dumb. Nobody, short of Einstein, could revise a physics text verbally. "Are you almost finished?"

"Oh no," Morris said hastily, "we have a lot left to do."

"It's really very exciting," Serena said eagerly. "I would so much like to see some of the text." She paused. "I enjoyed physics so much when I was in school." And put that in your pipe, she thought with a spurt of pleasure.

There was a blank silence for a moment then VanZandt said cheerfully, "We would love to show it off, but, unfortunately, there's a clause in our contract prohibiting us from showing it to anyone but the publisher. I suppose they're trying to make sure that we don't let portions get pirated."

"That's curious," Serena said with a total lack of inflection.

"Unusual, perhaps," VanZandt responded pleasantly. "Well, Serena, we really are enjoying our stay here at Castle Rock."

Morris smiled and nodded, then the two of them left.

Serena looked after them. Such charming, civilized men. She waited until they were out of sight then she hurried into the stables.

The professors were riding Black Alice and Jumping Joy. If they had been ridden as hard as the men claimed, they should still be grooming them. But the horses stood comfortably in their stalls, looking up to whinny as she came close. She leaned over the railing, touched Jumping Joy on his neck, ran a hand along his back. It was as cool and dry as windswept rock.

"Something wrong with Jumping Joy?"

Serena swung around, startled. Jed stood, hands on hips, watching her.

"No," she said flatly. "There's nothing wrong with Jumping Joy. He's quite cool. I'd say he hardly had a workout today."

"Who's riding him?"

"VanZandt."

"Well, I suppose the professors are too busy to spend much time riding." Jed's tone indicated a profound lack of interest in the topic.

"To the contrary," Serena said softly. "The professors told me they had ridden hard this afternoon."

Jed frowned. "But you say Jumping Joy . . ."

". . . has scarcely been ridden at all."

"I don't understand."

"Neither do I. But it sure makes me wonder what the professors did this afternoon to make them so hot and dirty."

She watched Jed closely, trying to read his expression. If he was one of the smugglers, and it made her feel sick to think of it, then he had to have help. This couldn't be a one-man show. She tried to interpret the sudden look of surprise that went as quickly as it came. Then he frowned and she had no difficulty recognizing sheer exasperation.

"For Christ's sake, Serena, are you busy playing detective?"

She didn't answer.

He reached out, gripped her arms so tightly they ached. "Stop it, Serena. Stop it. Or something bad may happen to you."

# Ten

"Come on, Danny, let's race," Serena shouted.

Danny didn't even take time to answer. Instead, he leaned low over Buster's neck, gave him a kick and the race was on.

Serena laughed, then she and Hurricane thundered after the small boy clinging like a burr to the back of his plunging horse.

The horses hooves' thundered and the world closed in to the feel of Hurricane beneath her and the sound of his breath, heavy and strained, and the whirling swirl of dust flowing up and around the two horses and the tearing pressure of wind in her face and the indescribable sense of elation welling up in her. As they thundered toward the corral, Serena called out, "The well pump," and she could see Danny nod.

Danny and Buster were just a nose ahead when they streaked by the rusted handle of the old well pump which had served so long to fill the troughs with water before electricity came to the ranch.

She and Danny reined in slowly, letting Buster and Hurricane ease from a gallop into a trot and then a walk. Both horses sides' heaved but their eyes glistened with excitement.

"I beat," Danny shouted. "I beat."

She reached over and squeezed his shoulder. "That was a good race, Danny, a wonderful race."

His face flushed with happiness. Danny smiled and she smiled, too. It was wonderful to see him looking like a little boy again, without a trace of strain or worry.

"Hey, Serena." Danny turned in his saddle to look at her. "Do you ride out to Castle Rock every day?"

She hesitated then nodded.

"Can I come along tomorrow like I did today?"

Again she hesitated, but so far, and she had been going for a week, Castle Rock looked just as it always had and she was beginning to think that her conviction that the mystery plane would return must be mistaken, so she nodded again. "Sure, Danny. You are always welcome."

They dismounted and cooled down their horses, cleaning and brushing until both shone like highly polished glass. Danny chattered on about the Fourth and the ribbon he was sure he would win and Serena listened, delighting in his pleasure and in the feel of Hurricane beneath her hands and the warmth of sunlight on her back. She was, she realized, gloriously happy, enjoying this afternoon as though none of the odd happenings which had clouded the summer mattered at all. Perhaps she was only imagining some of her fears. Perhaps they were the product of worry and grief. Perhaps everything was really all right. Everything seemed so right this afternoon. Not far away she could hear the blacksmith's hammer. The leaves of the huge cottonwood next to the corral rustled like dancer's slippers. Even the sound of someone, probably Peter or Mr. Minter, hitting golf balls on the range sounded pleasant and happy.

She finished grooming Hurricane first and turned to lead him into the stables. Danny was on one knee, checking Buster's left rear hoof.

"Hurry up, Danny, so we won't be late for dinner."

But she wasn't really in a hurry. She hated to see this lovely day come to an end, this day so touched with joy, so free of dark imaginings. She was smiling as she led Hurricane toward his stall. She was only a few feet into the stable when she stopped and looked around, her smile slipping away.

The horses were spooked. All of them. They moved uneasily in their stalls. Toward the back, in the stall next to Hurricane's, Devilwood was kicking the wall and the heavy ominous sound reverberated through the wooden stables like thunder.

"Devilwood!" she shouted.

Then Hurricane turned fractious, dancing sideways, pulling back against the halter. She gave a yank and, unwillingly, he came. The last ten yards to his stall, Hurricane twisted and pulled and it took all her strength to force him to come.

"Hurricane, what in the world is wrong with you?"

Perhaps a storm was coming. Sometimes the horses turned nervy when the dark heavy thunderclouds built up in the western sky. But the sky was clear this afternoon.

Serena sighed. Suddenly, she was tired and irritated and ready to be done with this. She gave another yank to Hurricane's halter, shoved open the door to his stall and stepped inside.

Hurricane's ears flattened. His nostrils widened. Abruptly, he reared, twisted and pulled free of her grasp.

"Hurri . . ."

She never finished.

Serena knew, of course, even before she looked down into the straw. The sound raised the hair from her skin, ran in hideous ripples in her mind, that frightful unmistakable dry husk of a sound.

The rattlesnake flicked his tail again and the high harsh warning rattle rasped in the dusty dim stall. Serena saw the undulating head, the dark raisin-shaped eyes, the deep indentations on either side of the snout. And she saw the flickering forked tongue. a tiny flash of flame in the dusky air.

In the next stall, Devilwood kicked the wall again.

The snake moved so rapidly, slithered in such a panic, that Serena could scarcely see the dark and sinuous body lunge across the straw then stop and rear, its head back to strike, only inches from her leg.

She stood in a macabre parody of the childish game of statues, one hand held high in the air, her breath a hard aching pressure in her lungs, her body rigid.

"Hey Serena, Buster has a rock in his shoe and I can't . . ." Danny's voice trailed off. "Hey Serena . . ."

Then the snake, his body puffing before her eyes, rattled his tail and the piercing warning exploded again.

Serena heard Danny's boots thudding down the aisle and his high scream for help, but she could only stand there, frozen in fear, her heart thudding unevenly, her eyes watching that blunt triangular head and the brilliant red tongue, a tiny flickering tongue of death. She breathed shallowly, each breath a victory.

Slowly, gradually, the snake sank back into a loose coil, alert but no longer poised to strike.

Sweat trickled down her face, but inside she felt cold as ice.

Could she step back? Did she dare move?

Devilwood stepped uneasily in the next stall and whinnied deep in his throat.

The rattler raised its head.

Such horribly empty eyes it had, so small and dark and un-blinking.

Slowly, with infinite patience, Serena lifted her left foot to take a backward step. She expected, of course, to step back onto the slightly downward sloping cement floor. The heel of her boot instead came down on the handle of a rake. She teetered for an instant, her balance lost, then, like a marionette yanked backward, she fell, landing hard on her hip. But she didn't even feel the pain that jolted through her.

She knew, had time to realize, that the snake was going to strike. She could hear, so near it sounded like a buzz saw, the frantic rattle of its rings. She glimpsed the snout in the air above her and the ruby red tongue and horror engulfed her. It was going to lunge at her throat and now there wasn't anything in the world she could do to save herself . . .

The roar of the rifle echoed in the closed building. Horses whinnied in fear and their hooves thundered against their stalls.

The snake, raised in full striking posture, hung headless in the dusky air for a long moment before it twisted and jerked and fell across Serena.

She screamed and screamed and screamed again.

Then Jed was there, using the rifle barrel to lift and toss away the still writhing body. Kneeling down, he caught Serena up in his arms. She clung to him shaking, tears streaming down her face.

"It's all right, it's all right," he murmured over and over again. She pressed against him, holding to warmth and safety, trying not to remember the feel of that hideous headless body as it fell across her.

"It's okay, Serena. Everything's all right. You don't have to be frightened now."

Finally, her breath still coming in uneven gulps, she pulled back to look up into his face. "If you hadn't come . . . if you hadn't . . ."

In the gloom of the stables, his face was white and drawn. "If Danny hadn't yelled . . ." He turned to look down at the rattler. "Godalmighty, he was striking. That damn snake was striking!"

"I got Jed," Danny was saying importantly, "I got Jed."

Yes, Serena thought weakly, if it hadn't been for Danny . . . She shuddered and looked at Jed. He was still staring down at the twisted body of the snake.

"That's good shooting," she said shakily.

"I'm a good shot," he said absently, but still he stared at the snake.

"You saved me."

Jed faced her then. "I might not be handy next time."

"Next time?"

His arm fell away from her, he rocked back on his heels. "Serena, you damn fool, I told you to stay out of this, but, no, you bull ahead . . ." He stopped, too furious to continue.

Yes, she thought miserably, he had warned her, hadn't he? Last night Jed told her to quit playing detective. That was what he said. And today, a rattlesnake lay in wait in Hurricane's stall.

If it hadn't been for Danny . . . Jed couldn't ignore Danny's shouts for help, not even if he knew the rattler was there.

Serena stared at Jed. Had he known? But surely his shot would have missed if he arranged the trap. Surely the fact that he killed the snake in the very act of striking proved his innocence?

Serena buried her face in her hands. She wished she could believe it. She wanted to believe it. Oh Jed, she cried to herself, it wasn't you. Don't let it be you. But, and she knew she must face it, Jed would have no choice once Danny screamed. Jed would have to come to the rescue. Anything else would betray him.

Serena's hands dropped from her face. Slowly, painfully, she began to get up.

Jed reached down and helped her stand.

"Ouch."

"What's wrong?" he asked sharply.

"Nothing bad. Just my hip. I tripped over something."

They both saw it then, lying at an angle to Hurricane's stall, a garden rake.

"How strange," Serena said slowly. "I suppose someone forgot to put it up . . ."

Jed shook his head. Then he bent and picked up a limp burlap sack lying in the shadows.

"Hey Jed," and Danny's voice was high and thin, "do you think somebody brought the rattler in here?"

"Yes," Jed said grimly.

"I'll bet it was Peter," Danny burst out. "He's the one who . . ."

"The one who what?" Peter's voice sounded lazy and casual, but it shocked the three of them into silence.

He walked nearer. "You all look like . . ." Then he saw the snake's body. "My God, where did that come from?"

"It was in Hurricane's stall," Serena said quickly. "Jed shot him."

"How the hell do you suppose he got in here?" Peter asked in amazement. "First time I ever heard of a rattler crawling in among a bunch of horses."

"It is a little strange, isn't it?" Jed agreed.

Peter gave the snake's body a kick with his boot. "Five feet long if he's an inch. I wouldn't have cared to meet up with him." Then he looked down at Danny, "What was it you were saying about me?"

Danny's chin jutted forward and he looked like a small stubborn edition of Uncle Dan. "I was going to say . . ."

"That you might have been the one who left the rake out," Serena interposed smoothly.

"The rake? No, that wasn't me though I did use it to rake out Victory's stall this morning." He looked intently at

123

Danny. "Why did you think I left it out?"

"Because you always leave things for other people to pick up," Danny said bluntly.

"I'll have to do better." Peter said lightly but his pale eyes were cold and angry.

Serena plunged in, hoping to distract Peter's attention from Danny. "Oh Peter, I've been meaning to talk to you. Will you and Julie present the trophies at the rodeo?"

"Rodeo?"

"You remember. Castle Rock always hosts a rodeo on the Fourth of July. Danny and Joe have made almost all the plans for this year."

"Ah yes," he drawled, "Silver cups for the cowboys. We will look forward to it with pleasure."

Danny glowered and Serena wished she hadn't asked Peter. His patronizing tone insulted all of them. She almost told him to forget it but she didn't want an open breach between herself and Julie's husband. They all lived on Castle Rock and it was important, especially for Danny, to keep things as pleasant as possible.

"Well, I'm glad you are none the worse for your meeting with the rattler," Peter said agreeably. Then, before any of them could object, he bent, picked up the rake and lifted the snake's body up on the prongs. "I'll clean this up." He turned and looked at Danny. "Guess I have to show I can do my part, too."

If there had been fingerprints on the rake, they would be smudged now. She read the same thought in Jed's eyes.

Peter was looking around the stables when he spotted the burlap sack in Jed's hand. "That's just the thing. Here, let's drop this fellow in there."

Silently, Jed held the sack open. Peter dropped in the snake's body. "Now, if you'll get rid of that, I'll get out Victory and Mademoiselle."

"Right," Jed said expressionlessly.

After Peter led the two horses out, Jed handed the sack to Danny. "Think you can get rid of this for us, Danny?"

"Sure." He hesitated, then asked, "Serena, do you think somebody put him in Hurricane's stall?"

"No," she said quickly, "it must have been an accident, Danny. Nobody would do something like that. The sack could have been there for a long time. As for the rake, well, things get left out all the time. Besides, no one could have known I would step back on it."

Danny frowned. "Snakes don't come around horses," he said stubbornly.

Serena managed a wry smile. "Maybe it was a dumb snake."

Danny laughed. "Yeah, a dumb snake." And he left, still smiling.

It was awkwardly quiet when Jed and Serena were left alone.

"Do you believe that?" Jed asked finally.

She shook her head.

"Why did you lie to Danny?"

"It wasn't exactly a lie," she said quickly. "It's just . . . Danny's so little, Jed. I don't want him to be frightened."

"Maybe it would be a good thing if he were a little scared . . . and you, too."

"I'm scared enough."

"Are you?" he asked harshly. He stepped closer, reached out and gripped her arms. "Serena, be careful."

She felt a rush of joy. He cared. He did care. It couldn't have been Jed who tried to hurt her . . .

Then he spoke again, his voice cold and rough. "Don't you know, Serena, accidents always come in threes?"

# Eleven

After it happened, Serena blamed herself. Why hadn't she expected something like this? Once it happened, the pattern seemed so clear, the objective so obvious.

The first accident happened to Uncle Dan—and it could only have been to prevent him from following up on the story told by the Burnt Hill hand of the plane which lifted off from Castle Rock.

The second accident happened to her—and it was after she had told all of them about the plane and Uncle Dan's fury and after she'd started trying to find out more about those who were on the ranch at the time, Jed and Will, and those lately come to the ranch who might be involved in future smuggling, the Minters and the professors.

She should have seen the pattern, the determination to prevent investigation but only through apparent accidents, never any overt violence.

She had, it was true, been cautious, keeping her bedroom door locked at night, checking the stables when she returned, watching out for any hint of danger on her morning rides to Castle Rock.

But she'd never expected what had happened.

She and Danny started breakfasting together every morning. Serena knew it gave him a sense of security to talk to her, to discuss the ranch and what Joe planned for the week. And, of course, every morning they talked about the Fourth.

Serena knew it had grown to glorious stature in Danny's imagination and she hoped he wouldn't be disappointed. It would, after all, be only a pick-up rodeo, even though the cowboys from the surrounding ranches and from Castle Rock were among the best in New Mexico. There would be some good rides, perhaps even some great rides. The bulldogging was always exciting and Danny still hoped to be allowed to compete in the calf-roping. The barbecue would be superb, Millie would see to that. The fireworks—Serena reminded herself that she must get into Santa Fe and buy fireworks that would make Danny proud of their show. Later in the week, she would do that.

So breakfast on Thursday, the week before the Fourth, followed the routine they had established.

When Serena finished her second cup of coffee, she said, "I'd better get to the office now."

Danny nodded. "Will we ride out about ten?"

That, too, was part of the routine.

"Sure, Danny."

"I'll bring Hurricane up."

But Danny never reached the stables that morning.

Serena was adding a long column of figures, thank God for calculators, and half-listening to the morning sounds of the ranch, the whir of the vacuum cleaner down the hall, the soft slap of a paint brush as one of the men put fresh white wash on the hitching post past the gate, and, high and steady like a windmill, the creak as Danny rode higher and higher on his rope swing.

She heard the creak, a summer sound, a part of her growing up, a cheerful constant rhythmic squeak, and suddenly, it stopped. She could see Danny in her mind, high in the air, the rope swinging like a pendulum. She knew even before he screamed.

Serena's chair toppled over backwards she moved so fast.

127

She slammed out of the office door, ran to the french windows and out onto the patio and then she stopped, her hand pressed against her mouth.

Danny lay in a crumpled heap amid the debris from the swing, the broken rope and the stuffed gunny sack.

He didn't move.

Serena ran, shouting for help as she did, then she dropped down beside him. Thank God, he was breathing. She put a hand gently on his chest, felt the slow rise and fall though his face was so waxen and still. She didn't dare move him. His back, his neck . . . She held his hands and prayed and waited for help.

Jed came, and he was wonderful, checking Danny gently. "His neck is all right, Serena. But . . ."

Danny stirred, making a low moan of pain.

"Don't move, Danny," Serena said quickly.

Danny's eyes opened. For a moment, they were blank and empty then Serena saw the fear come up in them. Her grasp tightened on his hands.

Jed fashioned a stretcher and supervised the careful move to the jeep. Serena stayed beside Danny. "I know it hurts, Danny." One leg was obviously broken. "We're going to fly into Santa Fe. Dr. Burris is waiting at the airport."

"I won't be able to ride Buster in the rodeo," Danny said faintly.

"Not this time. But one of these days."

He didn't cry. Not once. Not even when they jolted the stretcher unloading him at the airport. In the ambulance, he struggled to sit up.

Serena tried to push him down. "Danny, don't move so much. Not until they've done the X-rays."

"But Serena, I've never ridden in an ambulance before. Hey, listen to the siren."

That was when she started to relax, though she didn't feel really certain until Dr. Burris held up the X-rays. "There's a break in the femur but it's clean. I don't think he'll be in a cast more than a couple of months."

"A couple of months," Danny wailed.

"Listen, Danny," the doctor retorted, "you aren't made of rubber. Anybody that fell from the height you did should be thanking his lucky stars it wasn't far worse. What's a couple of months when you're going to be good as new?"

Danny slept on the flight back to the ranch. Serena felt uncomfortably aware of Jed's nearness in the quiet cockpit.

She would wait for him to speak first.

But he didn't.

Finally, she could stand it no longer.

"Jed, how do you suppose it happened?"

He didn't look at her. "The rope broke." His voice was colourless and unemphatic.

"Uncle Dan put the rope up. In May."

Jed checked the altimeter, adjusted his flight path.

"What are you saying, Serena?"

"I don't think it was an accident."

He stared straight ahead, his face grim. "We're almost there."

Serena looked away. So he wasn't going to talk to her about it at all. She felt tired and confused.

Jed landed the plane easily, as he did everything. The wheels touched, the plane lifted a little, then it touched again and rolled swiftly down the runway.

Will was there, waiting for them.

As the cockpit door opened, Will called out, "Hey Serena, how's Danny? Is Danny . . ." Then he saw Danny. "Hey pardner, you sure had us scared. What were you trying to do? Pretend you were Batman?"

Danny grinned up at his big cousin as he and Jed ma- noeuvred the stretcher out of the back of the plane.

Will carried Danny upstairs. Serena turned to thank Jed for flying them into Santa Fe, but he was gone. Wearily, she climbed the stairs.

Will was showing Danny how to use his crutches. "Put the weight on your hands, there in the crossbars, or you will get real sore under your arms. I know. I broke my leg in three places when I was a senior in high school."

"Gee, Will, how did you do that?"

"Playing football."

"I didn't know you played football."

"I didn't for long," Will said wryly, and Danny laughed.

Serena leaned against the door. She realized suddenly how tired she was and how frightened she had been. But it was going to be all right. She still remembered with dreadful clarity the waxy blue look on Danny's face when he lay unconscious on the patio. Dr. Burris had reminded her to keep a close watch on him for a few days. "It looks like a mild concussion, but you can never be sure. If he starts to sleep too heavily, if you can't rouse him, call me at once."

Will helped Danny to the bathroom. "Come on, pard, let me get some of that dirt off your face."

"Aw, Will."

Yes, Serena though grimly, she certainly did intend to keep a close watch over Danny. A very close watch.

It was probably a combination of exhaustion and the pain pills but Danny was asleep almost before they finished tucking him in. Will smiled, gently patted Danny's cheek, then turned to lead the way out.

Serena hesitated at the door.

"It's okay, Serry. He's sleeping like a log."

"I hate to leave him. The doctor said we need to keep a

close watch, make sure he doesn't sleep too heavily."

"Oh. Well look, I'll put up a cot and spend the night with him. I'm a light sleeper and I can check on him through the night."

"Oh, would you, Will?"

"Sure. But for now, let's go down and have a drink. You look all in."

As they went down the stairs and passed the ormolu-framed mirror in the foyer, Serena saw what Will meant. Her face was as white as the flowers of the magnolia tree. Dark smudges beneath her eyes made them look huge. In the den, she sank gratefully into a soft leather chair and watched while Will fixed drinks. He was squirting soda from a siphon when he looked up in concern. "Serena, did you have any dinner?"

She nodded. "Jed and I ate a sandwich at the hospital snack bar while they were putting the cast on Danny."

"Are you hungry? I could fix something up. I'm a pretty good cook."

She shook her head, smiling. It was funny to think of Will, so huge and muscular, busying around a kitchen.

He smiled down at her as he handed her the scotch and soda. Serena drank deeply, welcoming the smoky taste of the Chivas Regal. Then she looked around the empty room.

"Where is everybody tonight?"

Will pulled up a chair next to hers. "I don't know where the dudes are. I guess they just went back to their cabins after dinner. They knew Danny had been hurt."

"Where are Peter and Julie?"

"In Santa Fe. They were invited to a party at the Holmans."

"Oh." That was all Serena said.

"When the plane was still gone by mid-afternoon, they decided to drive into Santa Fe."

Not waiting, Serena thought coldly, to find out anything about Danny. A party at the Holmans was more important.

"Jed called back and said Danny was going to be okay," Will said quickly and Serena knew he had read her thoughts.

"I didn't know that. That was nice of him."

"Yeah."

Serena looked at him gravely. She hesitated, then asked bluntly, "Will, don't you like Jed?"

The lamplight shone on Will's flaming red hair but his face was in shadow. Then he turned toward her and she could see his strong jaw and firm chin. He was, she thought with a little shock of surprise, even handsomer than she had realized. Perhaps, she had not really looked at Will these last years.

"It isn't so much a question of liking or disliking," Will said slowly, his face solemn. "It's just . . . what do we know about him?"

Serena felt a fleeting pang of guilt. She knew that Jed had lied when he told her he received a degree from the University of Texas. There was no record of his graduating when he had said. No record at all. She should tell Will. She could confide in Will. He was part of Castle Rock, part of her life.

But she didn't.

Abruptly, she reached out and took Will's hand and held it tightly.

Will looked surprised, then delighted.

"Oh Will, I wish . . ."

"What do you wish, Serry?"

"I wish things could be the way they used to be."

"Maybe . . ." and he spoke with painful slowness, "maybe we can make things even better than they used to be." He was looking at her with so much love, so much concern.

Serena squeezed his hand once more then let it drop. "I

don't know, Will. I don't know what's going to happen to any of us. But I know you mean so much to me. I can trust you."

But even as she said it, she remembered Will's refusal to tell her what was worrying him at the start of the summer—and his weak explanation for having drunk too much the night before Uncle Dan died and the day of the funeral.

Wasn't this the time to clear it up, to ask him to tell her truthfully what was wrong? And to tell him of her suspicions?"

She almost did. Later, she would wonder if it would have made a difference? Would it have changed the future? Or was that future already certain, machinery once put in motion doomed to a foreordained end?

But she didn't ask. Will's happiness at being with her, the wonderfully warm sense of comfort she felt at his nearness, were too precious to risk. So she drew out the interlude, talking of this and that, of the ranch, of Will's paintings, of anything and everything but the strain and fear that permeated Castle Rock. And when they went upstairs, after she helped set up a cot for Will by Danny, when she stood once again outside Danny's door, Serena smiled at him then stood on tiptoe to lightly kiss his lips. "Goodnight, Will."

In her room, she undressed quickly, slipping into her gown. She kept thinking of Will. If Jed Shelton had never come to Castle Rock . . .

The soft knock on her door startled her. Then she hurried to her door. It must be Will. There was no one else upstairs. She yanked open the door, "Will."

It wasn't Will.

Jed stood there. He had heard her call Will's name. His eyes dropped to her gown. Serena flushed and drew the negligee close.

"Sorry," he said sardonically.

"Will's staying with Danny tonight. I was afraid something might be wrong," and she hated the defensive tone in her voice.

"Sure."

She could have slapped him.

"Look, I'll only take a minute," he continued. "I thought you might like to know about the rope."

"The rope?"

"The rope that was holding up the gunny sack."

She forgot her anger. "Yes," she said eagerly, "what about it?"

"Somebody burned it."

"Burned it," she repeated blankly.

And burned it, he meant. After bringing Danny up to the house, Jed had taken a flashlight and gone in search of debris from the swing. Millie told him it had all been dumped right inside the door to the tack room but when he went to look he found only the gunny sack. He searched among the ropes coiled in the tack room and even looked in the stables.

It was the smell that led him to the incinerator out behind the stables.

"You know how hemp stinks when it burns," he explained.

Anybody could have done it. It took only a minute to shove the rope into the incinerator, douse it with gasoline and toss in a match. Will could have done it. Or Julie. Or Peter. Or the Minters. Or the professors. Anybody at all.

"You don't seem shocked," Jed observed.

"I told you when we flew home," she said quietly. "I never thought it was an accident."

"But a little kid," he objected. "Who the hell would try to kill a little kid?"

The same person who killed Uncle Dan, she thought. Who tried to kill me. But she didn't say it. She just looked at him.

Jed frowned. "I don't understand why. I don't see it."

"Don't you? What would happen if Danny died?" she asked sharply.

He looked at her.

Serena laid it out. "Castle Rock would belong to Will and Julie, for one thing. For another, I would be booted out. And that's what the murderer wants."

There. She had said it. Murderer.

"Murderer?" he repeated. "Danny's going to be okay."

"Uncle Dan is dead."

"That was an accident."

"Funny, isn't it? So many accidents. All in a row. Uncle Dan's horse bolts. A rattlesnake shows up in Hurricane's stall. Danny's swing falls. Funny, isn't it?"

"No," he said harshly, "it isn't funny. Not a damn bit. My God, Serena, if that's what you think, why don't you get out of here?"

"I can't."

"Sure you can. Take a trip, Serena. Take Danny with you. Say you think he needs some sea air. Go to Galveston. Get the hell out."

He leaned forward, his face intent. He really wanted her to go, she was sure of that.

It would certainly simplify things for the smugglers if she left. Then there wouldn't be anyone trying to trap them, no one at all to stand in their way.

Wasn't the possibility that Uncle Dan had been killed as obvious to him as it was to her? And wasn't it Jed who warned her that accidents came in threes? If Jed were behind the accidents, he would make sure the rope was destroyed so there could be no evidence to take to the sheriff. Then he could use the very act of the rope's destruction as a way to try and frighten her more and drive her from the ranch.

"I'll fly you down to Padre Island tomorrow," he said eagerly.

"No."

"Serena, you have to get out of here."

"No," she said defiantly. "I belong here. I'm going to stay here."

He glared at her. "You little fool. I tell you I know what I'm talking about . . ."

He broke off and they stared at each other, Serena in shock, Jed in confusion.

"What do you know?" she asked steadily.

His mouth twisted. "I know stupidity when I see it."

Suddenly Will loomed up behind Jed. "Hey Serena, is everything all right? I heard loud voices." He looked from her to Jed and Serena knew he would love to manhandle Jed right out of her room. She saw too the flash of anger in Jed's eyes. He would explode if Will touched him.

Serena stepped between them, put a hand on Will's arm. "Everything's fine. You'd better get back to Danny. Is he sleeping all right?"

"I just checked him," Will said, not taking his eyes off Jed.

The two of them glared, much like angry dogs circling in a barnyard.

"It's all right, Will," she said insistently. "You go back to bed now."

He left finally, his face still truculent. When Danny's door shut behind him, Jed asked abruptly, "Is he why you're staying at Castle Rock?"

"Will?" Serena said in surprise. "What makes you think that?"

"I was coming up the stairs to tell you about the rope and I saw you kiss him."

He didn't go on to say that then, at his knock, she had

opened her door in her negligee saying Will's name, but she could read it in Jed's eyes.

Serena lifted her chin. "I grew up with Will," she said steadily. "I care very much for him. I see no reason why I shouldn't kiss him goodnight."

"Do you call that a goodnight kiss?" Jed said derisively. He stared down at her, then, abruptly, he pulled her into his arms and his mouth sought hers. She struggled, trying to turn away but he held her immovable against him and his lips found hers in a violent, demanding, explosive kiss. She responded, her mouth opening, her heart beginning to pound.

When he let her go as abruptly as he had pulled her close, he glared down at her. "That's a goodnight kiss," he said angrily, then he turned on his heel and was gone.

# Twelve

Julie wore white walking shorts and a crisp blue cotton blouse. Her shining blonde hair swung in a ponytail. She looked about sixteen and, Serena thought enviously, absolutely beautiful. Serena felt like warmed-over cat food. She had slept poorly and felt the beginnings of a headache.

Julie perched on the edge of Uncle Dan's desk. "Serena, you hardly seem to come out of the office at all anymore."

Serena leaned back in her chair. "There's so much to take care of," she said wearily.

Julie lifted her hands above her head, stretched like a lithe kitten, then smiled. "I have a marvellous idea. Let's get away for a while."

"Get away?" Serena put down her pen and stared at Julie.

"Yes. You're working too hard and I'm bored to pieces." She clapped her hands together. "I know what let's do! Let's fly to Dallas and go shopping."

It did, for an instant, sound absolutely lovely. To wander about Neiman-Marcus and all the small specialty shops. To eat dainty lunches and drink white wine and be far away from the sullen brooding atmosphere of the ranch. It did, for an instant, sound grand.

Then Serena asked quietly, "Who put you up to this, Julie? Was it Jed's idea?"

A look of pure surprise washed over Julie's face. "Oh no, Serena. What makes you think that?"

Serena looked at Julie's lovely face—and remembered how Julie excelled at acting. She was perfectly capable of lying while looking like an angel.

"Oh, I don't know," Serena said slowly. "I just thought he might have suggested it to you."

"Why should he care what you do?" Julie asked innocently.

"No reason at all," Serena said quickly.

Julie tilted her head. "He is cute, isn't he?"

"I suppose so," Serena said woodenly. "I hadn't really noticed."

Julie laughed at that, lightly, charmingly. "Oh my dear, hadn't you really?"

After Julie left, Serena stared at the letter she was writing for a long, long time. She started over twice, then crumpled up each sheet in a tight ball and threw it viciously at the wastebasket. Her head was killing her. Abruptly, she shoved back her chair. Usually she worked in the office until ten, then she saddled up Hurricane. But this morning she wanted out in the open now to try and ease the tight muscles in her neck. She would ride Hurricane like the wind and the fresh air sweeping against her face would make her feel good again, banish the tight hard knot of anger.

Serena hurried down the path to the stables, not making any effort to be quiet but running lightly on the gravel. She decided to check Hurricane before she went into the tack room. She plunged into the dim light of the stables and it was like diving into a pool of dark water. She loved the quiet and the smell of horses and hay. Hurricane looked over the edge of his stall and whinnied. She realized she had forgotten to bring a carrot. She slipped her arms around his neck and pressed her cheek against his head. Dear, dear Hurricane. He stood very still, welcoming her caress.

139

She heard voices then and realized somebody must be in the tack room.

"Damn," Serena said softly.

She didn't want to talk to anyone. Not now. She wanted to be alone on the trail. Then she stiffened and strained to hear.

Julie's voice carried well. "But Jed, why did you want me to ask her? It wouldn't be any fun if she came along."

"Peter wouldn't think anything of it if you and Serena went shopping and I flew you. He might look at it a little differently if you and I went alone."

Every word carried so clearly, so devastatingly, and every word made it clearer and clearer that Jed and Julie knew each other better than anyone guessed. The arms that had held Serena, the mouth that had pressed against hers, knew Julie too, knew her well.

Julie's voice was muffled now. "Jed, it couldn't be that you are just the teeniest little bit interested in Serena, could it?"

Serena heard his answer and her face flamed in the dim stable light. "Hey Julie, are you jealous? I'll have to spend more time with Serena if it has such a nice . . ."

His voice broke off and Serena knew Julie was kissing him.

That was when Serena turned and fled. She burst out of the stables and ran toward the hacienda. She gained her room without seeing anyone, but she found no peace there. She paced up and down the long lovely room, past the row of Kachinas and back again. The devils that rode her clung and pained. Abruptly, her mouth thin, she lifted her small travelling case down and quickly packed. Then, still moving fast, wild to be gone, she pulled off her boots, kicked off her Levis and shirt and dressed for town.

In the hall, she paused at Danny's door, then opened it to look in. He was asleep, sandy lashes dark against his pale face. The cast looked huge. Serena gently closed the door. It was good for him to sleep. She would call and talk to him when she reached Santa Fe.

But, before she left, she must talk to Joe Walkingstick.

She found him in the west pasture, working on a leaky stock tank. He saw her Mustang coming and climbed down to wait. When she pulled up, he was mopping his face. "Hot," he said simply.

"Is it coming okay?" she asked.

"Sure. I'll have it fixed by this afternoon." Then he looked at her curiously. "You going into town?"

"Yes. I have some things to attend to. I'll stay at La Fonda."

"When will you be back?"

"In a day or two. I'll pick up the fireworks for the Fourth and the prizes for the rodeo." But she made no move to go. Joe waited, his dark eyes alert. He didn't ask. He never wasted words.

"Joe."

He looked at her intently, realizing from her tone that she had something out of the ordinary to say.

"Joe, I want you to promise me that you will look after Danny."

"Danny?"

She told him then, everything she knew or surmised. His face never changed expression but, when she finished, he nodded once and she knew, without question or comment, that Joe would do his best, that Danny would be safe.

So she didn't worry, not all the way down to Santa Fe, not during a peaceful afternoon as she wandered down narrow streets, looking at paintings and sculpture and pottery. She didn't worry and she tried very hard not to think about Castle Rock at all. She made several calls, arranging for shipment of the fireworks and ordering a silver-trimmed saddle as the grand prize and a number of bridles and belt buckles as secondary prizes. She enjoyed her dinner at the old hotel, enjoyed being alone and watching the other guests, wondering where they came from and what brought them to Santa Fe, an old city which had seen conquistadors and friars, outlaws and lawmen, peaceful Indians and warriors, and, of late years, artists and writers of all persuasions, many superb and many mediocre. After dinner, she stopped in the bar for one more drink then walked slowly upstairs to her room.

She lay sleepless but dry-eyed for a long time, watching the arc of the moon in the movement of shadows across her ceiling, and she thought of herself and Peter and Will and Jed.

Twice now, she had opened her heart to treachery. Did she have a weakness, a lack of judgment that doomed her to betrayal?

It could happen once to any woman. Once, perhaps, it must happen to every woman. She had been lonely when Peter came and he was so handsome. But she had not, in any real sense, committed herself to Peter so his annexation by Julie hadn't broken her heart. It did make her doubt her own perceptiveness because she had thought, until the very end of the summer, that he cared for her. And she knew that really it hadn't been Julie's doing. Oh yes, she had flirted with Peter. Julie flirted with any man, every man, but somehow Peter had cared for Serena one day and the next for Julie.

Was the true attraction Castle Rock? Had Peter discovered that Serena was only Dan McIntire's ward, that she had no claim on Castle Rock?

Serena bunched a pillow behind her head and watched the shifting shadows above her.

If that had been the case, then Dan McIntire's will must have infuriated Peter.

Although that could have been the reason for Peter falling

away, how did she account for Jed?

She had been so sure, so positive, that Jed cared for her. So certain.

Once again in her mind she heard Julie's soft husky voice, the rustle of her dress, and the sudden cessation of Jed's words because Julie was kissing him.

So she had been wrong. One more time. Maybe Jed liked to kiss all the ladies, although she could have sworn . . . But, obviously, she had pretty lousy judgment as far as men were concerned.

Well, she had a ranch to run and a boy to protect. Horrible to think that someone at Castle Rock, someone she knew, would be willing to sacrifice Danny's life to get Serena off the ranch. At least Danny was safe for now, secure in his room.

Serena sighed. She couldn't hide here in Santa Fe, grieving for a love that hadn't been. She must go back to Castle Rock and try to meet the threat that moved unseen across the ranch.

Will would help her. She could count on Will. With Will and Joe, she would face the danger down, keep Danny safe, make Castle Rock the happy haven it had always been.

She would leave love for another time, perhaps another place.

Will would help her . . .

So sleep came finally and, deep in her mind, she clung to that thought, Will would help her.

The phone rang shrilly.

Serena struggled against the heavy hotel spread and came flailing awake, uncertain for a moment where she was, frightened by the loud demanding ring in the dark room. She reached up, grabbed up the receiver and came wide-awake at the sound of Will's voice.

"Serena, oh Serena, I hate to tell you this."

"Will, what is it?"

"Danny's gone."

She didn't answer. She couldn't. The enormity of his words left her stunned.

"There isn't a trace of him," Will continued in a rush. "We've looked everywhere, upstairs, downstairs, in the cellar, in the outbuildings. God, we've looked everywhere!"

"Oh no. Oh Will, no."

"Serena, I'm so sorry. I never thought . . . I didn't stay with him last night. I wanted to but he said no. I guess he thought it was babyish. And I knew his head was okay. He hadn't had any trouble all day. I told him he could call me on the house-phone if he needed anything and he said sure. He was so chipper. He'd been around on his crutch all day like a monkey. God, I never thought . . ."

"He can't be missing," Serena insisted. "He can't."

"He is."

And nothing could change a word of it. Millie had taken in his breakfast tray and wakened everyone when she couldn't find him.

"When you say everyone got up," Serena said sharply, "was everyone in bed?"

"In bed? Oh, I guess not really. Joe was already up and down at the corral. Jed, too. They were getting ready to take some hands and go check the cattle in Big East. Instead, they helped search the house."

"Where were Julie and Peter?"

"Asleep. But they got up and helped look. So did the Minters and the professors. We all looked. Everybody's still looking but I came in to call the sheriff and you."

The sheriff. She must talk to him, tell him what she knew, what she guessed. She had no proof of anything. But wasn't

144

the fact that Danny was missing a terrible kind of proof that something was wrong at Castle Rock?

"All right, Will. You stay in charge. Send out search parties. Especially to Castle Rock. Call the Circle Bar M and Burnt Hill and Crazy Horse. They'll send riders to help. We'll find Danny."

"Sure, Serena. We'll find him."

Neither of them gave flesh to the spectre that haunted their thoughts. They would find Danny, find him alive. They wouldn't even think it could be any other way.

"Tell the sheriff everything you know, Will. And I'll be home as fast as I can."

She didn't stop for breakfast. She grabbed coffee to go in a styrofoam cup and a doughnut and the Mustang was wheeling north fifteen minutes after Will called. As the road lifted and curved, past scrub brush, sage and skunkweed, Serena kept looking to the west and the thick puffy clouds, like a tufted gray quilt, that hung on the horizon. If those clouds darkened and swelled into oily black mounds, it could presage a New Mexico cloudburst—and Danny must be found before then.

All the long way back to the ranch, Serena drove furiously, her face white and set, her thoughts angry and self-recriminatory. She never should have left Danny behind. Never.

But she had felt so secure with Joe on the look-out. Who would ever have thought Danny might disappear in the middle of the night? Certainly it had never occurred to her. And there was no reason to blame Joe. She had warned him to protect Danny against "accidents." His disappearance couldn't be considered an accident. It was kidnapping. But to what end?

Serena was terribly afraid she knew the answer.

She drove recklessly across the ranch, dust boiling behind her. She skidded the Mustang to a stop beside a police van parked next to the stables. Sheriff Coulter stood, hands on his hips, his sunburned face creased in a frown, listening to a deputy.

Serena caught the end of the deputy's sentence ". . . sure as hell looks like an inside job to me, Sheriff."

Sheriff Coulter frowned. "You didn't find any sign of forced entry?"

"No. Nothing. Not a scratch anywhere." The deputy added a little defensively, "If anybody broke into this house last night, I'll eat my hat."

"All right, Tom," the sheriff said mildly. "If you couldn't find it, I'd guess it wasn't there." He sighed. "Get pictures of the kid's room. The door. The windows."

The deputy looked surprised. "But this isn't a homicide . . ."

Sheriff Coulter interrupted sharply, "We don't know what the hell it is. Get the pictures." Then he looked past the deputy and nodded to Serena. "I'm glad you're back, Serena. I want to talk to you. Just a second and let me check on what's happening." He poked his head into the back of the van. "Has anything come in?"

"No," a man's voice answered. "The search party has reached Castle Rock. They're poking around in the caves but they haven't spotted anything to indicate he might be there. The other parties are working their areas but don't have anything to report."

"Okay. I'm going up to the house with Miss Mallory. Call me if you hear anything."

"Yes, sir."

The sheriff backed out the van and turned to join Serena. "Do you have a quiet spot where we can visit?"

146

"My office. And Sheriff, I have a lot to tell you."

He looked at her sharply. "Is it anything that will help the search? I have six parties out there now."

"No. If I had any idea where he was, I'd certainly tell you. But I may know why he was taken."

Once in her office with the door closed behind them, Serena told her long story. When she described the plane that the Burnt Hill hand had seen, the sheriff exploded, "Why the hell didn't you call me?"

Serena looked away from his angry face. "I suppose I was trying to handle it myself because . . . if someone in the family was involved, I thought perhaps I could stop it, scare them away from coming back."

"Just pretend it never happened?"

Slowly she nodded. "Then when I thought maybe Uncle Dan had been killed . . ."

"Dan killed?"

Serena explained how she had reasoned it out, Dan McIntire riding out to look again at Castle Rock, someone lying in wait for him, then, as Uncle Dan started to dismount, a rifle shot, a bolting horse and an "accident."

"But, Serena, what could the landing of a smuggler's plane and even Dan's murder have to do with Danny being kidnapped now?"

So she told him in a dry and brittle voice of how she had told everyone of the plane and how the very next day Julie had sent her away from Castle Rock. "But Uncle Dan left it in his will for me to run Castle Rock and take care of Danny. So I came back to the ranch and the next week there was a rattle-snake in Hurricane's stall."

"Who could have put it there?"

"Anyone. Everyone. I rode out on Hurricane every day with Danny. Everyone knew that."

"But the rattler didn't get you."

"It almost did."

"Why didn't you call me then?" he asked angrily.

"Murder by snake?" she asked wryly. "I didn't think anyone would believe that. But I should have come to you when Danny was hurt—someone burned the rope."

"Another accident," the sheriff said heavily. "Who found the rope?"

"Jed Shelton."

"Jed Shelton. Isn't that the new young fellow?"

Serena nodded.

"Wasn't he flying the Aerocommander when you found Dan's body?"

"Yes."

"Was he here on the ranch when the Burnt Hill hand saw that plane take off?"

"Yes." Then she added levelly, "So was Will."

The sheriff shot her a quick little look of surprise and she felt colour mounting in her cheeks.

The sheriff lit a cigarette, drew the smoke in deeply. "All right, let's leave that for the moment. Let's get back to Danny. Why would anybody take Danny away? What would that have to do with any of the rest of this?"

"It's simple enough," she said wearily. "I'm a danger because I know about the smuggling—and I won't drop it. I think another shipment must be coming in soon and they're afraid that somehow I will ruin it. If nothing else, they know I'm watching and looking. So they want me off the ranch. The rattlesnake didn't get me. But if anything happens to Danny, the ranch will belong to Will and Julie—and Julie would kick me off the ranch the minute she could."

The sheriff looked at Serena in shocked surprise. "Why?"

She didn't have any intention of telling the sheriff about

Jed and Julie. "For a lot of reasons," Serena said tautly.

"So you think the smugglers know this and they're willing to kill Danny just to get rid of you?"

"Yes." Serena buried her face in her hands. "There's no reason to hope that he's alive. No reason at all."

"My God," the sheriff said bleakly.

"I shouldn't have left him," she cried, "not even for a minute. But I thought he was safe. I told Joe. I warned him to look out for accidents. But I never thought . . ."

The sheriff reached out, gently took her shoulders in his huge hands and shook her until she looked up at him.

"Serena, you've got to tell me. Who's behind it? You must have some idea. It's too late now to protect anybody." His hands tightened. "You have to tell me."

# Thirteen

Serena looked at the sheriff with stricken eyes. "You're right," she said huskily. "I can't protect anyone. It's Danny's life, isn't it?"

The sheriff loosened his grip but he nodded grimly. "If he's out there alive, Serena, we have to find him soon. The thunderheads are building up. It's just a matter of time now. And if he's anywhere on low ground . . ."

He didn't have to tell her. Serena knew New Mexico, knew the gritty gray dusty arroyos that could turn into channels of raging red foam, conduits of water gone mad. When a big storm broke, water swept in blinding sheets, water falling so heavily it bruised and battered, wild and uncontrollable water tearing trees and boulders from the ground.

If Danny were on low ground . . .

Oh, how they clung to hope. To the idea of Danny, a little boy with sandy hair and green eyes and a happy heart, somewhere alive.

But if the person who had loosed a rattler and tampered with a rope had Danny, how could they hope?

Two images mingled in her mind, that of Danny, open faced and laughing, and that of Jed, his steady eyes looking into hers with what she had thought was love.

She had begun to care for Jed, care more than she ever had before. Surely he couldn't have taken Danny, surely it wasn't Jed.

But Jed lied when he told her of his past and he made love to her as if he really cared but all the while he was loving Julie, too. So it couldn't have been love at all. And if she was wrong about that, she could be wrong about him in so many ways.

A knock sounded on the office door.

"Come in," Serena called out.

It was Jed.

He nodded at her. "Glad you've made it back." Then he looked at the sheriff. "Is there any word on Danny?"

"No, nothing. How about? Did you find anything from the air?"

Jed shook his head. "I've flown over the whole ranch. There's nothing out of the ordinary. No strange cars, no trespassers, nothing. Then the turbulence began to get bad and I came in."

"The storm's still building?" Serena asked anxiously.

"Yes," Jed replied. "It's coming. I'm going to take one more sweep then it'll be too rough."

Serena looked at Jed and felt her heart breaking. He stood only a few feet from her but she felt the distance between them was too far ever to be bridged. His face was weary and drawn. You could see the concern and caring in his eyes. But could you, she wondered bitterly? Was what she saw really there or was it emotion of her own making?

He felt her eyes on him and looked toward her.

"I've told the sheriff everything," she said flatly, almost angrily.

Did he look wary, or did she imagine that? He answered equably enough. "That's good."

"I told him how you found the rope from Danny's swing burning."

Jed waited and now he did look wary.

The sheriff looked from one to the other.

151

"You warned me that accidents come in threes," she continued.

Jed's mouth tightened into a thin grim line.

"You wanted me to go away from the ranch, didn't you, Jed?" She had started now. She wasn't going to stop. "You asked Julie to try and talk me into going to Dallas, leaving the ranch."

"That true, young man?" the sheriff demanded.

Slowly, Jed nodded.

"Why did you do that?" the sheriff asked gruffly.

"I thought Castle Rock was a dangerous place for Serena to be. That's why."

"So it was just for my well-being," she said sarcastically.

"Just that." Red tinged his cheeks.

"Good of you."

They glared at each other now, both openly angry.

"If you'd gone, Danny might be okay," Jed said furiously.

"What do you mean by that?" the sheriff barked.

"I mean someone is damned anxious to get Serena away from here, one way or another. Maybe if she'd gone away for awhile, Danny would be all right."

"If you know anything about Danny's disappearance . . ." the sheriff began ominously.

"I don't know a damn thing more than you do. And I'm trying my damndest to find him." With that Jed swung on his heel and slammed out of the office.

Serena looked after him with an anguish she couldn't hide.

"So that's what you think," the sheriff said quietly.

Slowly, painfully, she nodded.

"Why, Serena? He looks a fine young man. Why do you think he's the one?"

"Nothing like this ever happened until he came—and he came from nowhere."

She told the sheriff how Jed had come to the ranch and about the time she found him looking through Will's room and how the University of Texas didn't have him listed as a graduate though he'd said he was.

"That's enough to make you wonder," the sheriff agreed. "All right, Serena, I'll get to work on it, see what I can find out about him."

"Yes," she said quietly, "I think you should. And Sheriff, he could be in league with either the Minters or the professors." She described her suspicions of them all. The sheriff was especially interested in the gun she had seen in the Minters' closet.

"In a holster?" he asked.

"Yes. It was a big hand-gun. A dark blue one."

The sheriff looked at her sombrely. "I don't suppose I have to warn you to be careful?"

"No."

"I'm going to anyway. Don't trust anyone. And if you come up with any other ideas, come to me."

When the sheriff left, Serena stood for a moment by Uncle Dan's desk. She held onto the back of his high black chair, wishing so much that he could be there. He wouldn't let harm come to Danny. Uncle Dan had been so big and strong. But he was dead. If the person who engineered his death was behind Danny's disappearance . . . But she wouldn't think of that, she wouldn't let horror take root in her mind and grow. They were going to find Danny. They were.

She slammed out of the office and hurried to the kitchen. Millie was packing lunches.

"Oh Serena, I'm so glad you're back. I thought Joe would come back and help with the lunches but he hasn't. Can you take the food out to the search parties in the pick-up?"

"Yes, I'll do that." Serena began to help wrap the sandwiches. It kept her hands busy. It was something to do, little enough, to help in the search for Danny.

"You haven't heard anything, Millie?"

"Not yet. But they will find him. Don't worry, Serena."

Millie sounded so confident and unworried that Serena looked at her in surprise.

Millie smiled. "Joe told me the Kachinas will look out for Danny. He will be all right."

The Kachinas. Millie meant the supernatural beings that Hopis call upon to help corn grow and people conceive, to banish illness and fear. The Kachina dolls in her room upstairs represented both the gods and the dancers who impersonated the deities. Serena had grown up going to their dances and she had vivid memories of drumbeats and the clap of gourds and the rattle of silver bells on frosty night air or in midday heat and the stately processions of dancers in their feathers and finery.

Although Millie was moving quickly around the kitchen, intent upon her tasks, hurried, there was an aura of peace, a serenity that for an instant touched Serena with hope. Danny was a living force in that kitchen, alive and, somewhere, safe.

The Kachinas will keep him safe.

God, how she hoped Millie was right.

But the Kachinas were only dolls upstairs in her room or masked dancers at the pueblo. They couldn't protect a little boy from evil.

It was almost as if she had spoken aloud. Millie turned, her dark face furrowed and uneasy. "Serena, I did want to tell you. There is evil here at Castle Rock."

Serena started to answer that yes, she knew, but Millie was looking carefully toward the door, then she gestured for Serena to come. She unlocked a small door beyond the freezer and led the way into a wood-floored pantry. She walked to the corner and began to pull a green trash sack toward the light. She held the lips of the bag closed.

"I hate to show you, Serena, but Joe said I must when you got back from Santa Fe."

She opened the sack.

Serena stared down in shock at the stiff body, the legs rigid, the greenish eyes staring upward.

"Mr. Richard," Serena cried, looking down at the dead cat, his magnificent orange and white fur now so limp and pathetic. Danny's cat. A huge battered-eared tom who had the run of the ranch. He always spent the night at Danny's feet. Serena looked up at Millie in horror. "What happened to him?"

The Indian woman shook her head. "I don't know. I found him dead on Danny's bed when I took up his breakfast."

Had Danny seen Mr. Richard dead and been upset and perhaps run away . . . ? No, she was forgetting. Danny's leg was broken. He couldn't run anywhere. But how odd that his cat should die the very night Danny was kidnapped.

Odd?

More than that, of course. It couldn't be a coincidence. That was asking too much of credulity. No. Mr. Richard, then, hadn't died a natural death. Serena looked again at the stiff body, trying to understand why and how a child's pet would be killed. What could possibly be the point of it?

"Millie, what did Joe say about the cat?"

Millie frowned. "He said," she began slowly, "to be sure and tell Serena that Mr. Richard was killed and to . . ."

"Did he say killed?" Serena interrupted sharply.

Millie thought for a moment, then nodded decisively.

"That is just what he said, to tell you that Mr. Richard was killed and you should be very careful and he would explain later."

155

"Where is Joe now?"

"Out with the searchers."

Serena looked again at the dead cat as if the very fact of his death should speak to her, tell her something, make clearer the obscure and frightening occurrences at Castle Rock.

Millie followed her gaze. "He was fine last night when I took Danny his supper. I had to shoo him away when he tried to eat Danny's steak."

Mr. Richard always believed that anything Danny had belonged to him, too. So the cat had been alive and well last night.

When had he died?

It must, of course, have been something in his food.

Serena stood very still, an idea glimmering in her mind. Mr. Richard's food?

"Millie, when did Mr. Richard eat?"

"In the mornings. 'Course, he always snacked at night with Danny . . ."

"Millie," she asked excitedly, "what did you feed Danny last night?"

Millie lifted her chin. "My food is good food, Serena. Nothing I fixed could have hurt Danny."

Serena reached out, touched her arm. "I know that. Of course, I know that. But I have an idea. Quick, Millie, tell me everything you fixed last night."

"A club steak and mashed potatoes and gravy and peas. And I made a strawberry shortcake with lots of whipped cream. It was good food."

Serena frowned. Nothing could be put into a steak and it would be hard to do with the vegetables.

"The drink. What did Danny drink?"

"A Coke. In a can. He likes to drink from the can."

A cat will eat steak and perhaps lick gravy and even sometimes chew a few peas. But cats don't drink Coke.

"Is that all, Millie? Are you sure that's all?"

Millie started to nod then paused. "Oh well, that's everything at dinner."

"But after dinner?" Serena asked gently.

"I took Danny some warm milk about ten o'clock and told him it was time to turn off the TV."

Warm milk.

Danny didn't like milk. Warm or cold. Had never liked it. Wouldn't drink it.

Cats love warm milk.

She could see a possible answer now.

"Millie, I want you to tell me everything you did with the milk. Everything."

Serena led her through it, Millie frowning all the while, the pouring of the milk into the saucepan, the wait until it almost began to boil, the dash of vanilla.

"Then I put it in a mug and carried it up and put it by his bed."

"Then what happened?"

"I waited until his programme was over then I helped him into the bathroom . . ."

"When you went to the bathroom, could someone have come into Danny's room without your seeing them?"

Millie thought about it. "Yes," she said finally, "someone could have. Danny had some soap bubbles and he blew them."

If someone had seen Millie go upstairs carrying the tray with milk on it then waited a moment in the hall, the watcher could have seized the chance to finish the job begun when the swing was sabotaged.

"Did you see Danny drink any of the milk?"

"No. He said he would drink it in a little while. So I kissed him goodnight and came back downstairs."

Serena nodded. In her mind, she could see Danny falling asleep with the big orange-and-white cat in his arms. Then, he would move in his sleep and the cat would wriggle free and stretch and stand up to move about. Did Mr. Richard smell the milk? If he found it, he would crouch beside the mug, his pink tongue lapping greedily.

"All right, Millie. I think I know what happened. I'm going to tell the sheriff about Mr. Richard."

Serena hurried out of the kitchen, knowing that Millie watched her go with frightened eyes. But it would be well for her to be frightened. They all should be frightened.

Sheriff Coulter listened intently. Then, his face grim, he turned to a deputy. "Go get that cat and take it into town for an autopsy. Pronto."

Serena went with the deputy to the kitchen and told Millie it was all right for him to take Mr. Richard. Then, with Millie's help, she loaded the back of the pick-up with lunches for the searchers. She drove the pick-up across the ranch at sixty miles an hour, dust boiling in her wake like smoke from a brushfire.

As she found each group, she honked and they gathered round, glad to pause for a moment from the grueling ride, drinking deeply of the icy water in the huge tin drum before reaching out for their sandwiches. Each time, she would look hopefully at the leader, but the answer was always the same; nothing, no trace, nothing.

All the while, the clouds boiled blackly in the western sky. The thunderheads moved nearer and nearer and the air hung hot and heavy, the sultry harbinger of the coming storm. By the time she pulled back into the parking area behind the stables, the sky overhead was darkening. Thunder rumbled in the mountains.

Serena hurried up to the house. Julie waited on the front porch.

"Serena, where have you been?" Julie's face was pale and drawn and, for the first time in a long time, Serena felt close to her. Julie too loved Danny. She was obviously upset.

"I took food out to the search parties. Has there been any word?"

Julie shook her head. "Not a damned thing. I tell you, Serena, this is driving me crazy."

"I know," Serena said sympathetically, "but we have to hope, Julie. They will find him. They will."

Julie looked at her blankly, then said jerkily, "Do you think so? You're a fool then. Nobody kidnaps some kid then lets them be found. What I don't understand is why we haven't had some kind of note or telephone call." She led the way into the hacienda, looking back at Serena. "And where are all those deputies? Why aren't some of them up here guarding us? I tell you, Serena, we ought to demand protection."

Protection. So that was what Julie was concerned about. Of course. She was worried about herself. Not about Danny. Not about a little boy taken from his bed in the middle of the night.

Serena ignored Julie as they walked into the den. The middle of the night. Why hadn't Danny shouted, called out for help? His cousin Will was only two doors away. His cousin Julie and her husband were so close.

Why hadn't Danny called out?

". . . and I'm getting out of here. I told the sheriff I was going but he said I had to stay until they knew what happened to Danny. But I think that's crazy. Why, we could all be dead in our beds . . ."

"Shut up, Julie."

Julie's head jerked up.

159

"That's right," Serena said clearly. "I said shut up. Stop thinking about yourself for five minutes. Nobody's trying to hurt you."

That was important, too, Serena thought suddenly. There had been no threat to Julie or Will, only to Danny and Serena. That told her something didn't it? Of course. The focus of everything was control of Castle Rock. Once you understood that, it all made sense.

Danny and Serena. Serena and Danny. A rattlesnake. A broken swing. A dead cat. That could never have passed as an accident, could it? But someone could have said, look, it happens all the time, somebody in pain, they take too many . . .

Serena turned and ran from the room, hurrying up the stairs toward Danny's room.

# Fourteen

The deputy was young. Her age. No older. But he stood his ground doggedly.

"Sorry, Miss. The sheriff said nobody was to go in that room. Nobody."

Serena bit her lip in frustration. She was wild to see that bedside table. Then the sheriff spoke behind her.

"So here you are, Serena."

"Sheriff," she said quickly, "I need to see Danny's room. I've figured out what must have happened and I want to see if his pain pills are there beside his bed."

"All right," and he motioned the deputy to step aside.

Serena paused for an instant on the threshold. Danny's model airplanes hung motionless from their silken threads tacked to the ceiling. He had just finished the Spirit of St Louis a week ago. His soccer ball and cleats were kicked carelessly in a corner. Three rows of Hardy boy books filled a bookcase. The crumpled covers on the bed looked as if he might just have thrown them back.

Serena took a deep breath and forced herself to walk to the bedside table. The medicine bottle was there, shiny brown plastic with the neatly typed legend on white stickum paper: TAKE EVERY FOUR HOURS FOR PAIN, DO NOT EXCEED DOSAGE.

The bottle was full when the prescription was filled. Two pills remained. She turned and saw the sheriff nodding in unspoken agreement.

"In the milk," she whispered.

"The autopsy on the cat showed codeine."

Serena looked back down at the night table. "There isn't any glass. Did Millie take it down to the kitchen this morning?"

The sheriff shook his head. "No. She said she didn't even think about the glass when she found Danny missing."

"Then where can it be?"

"I imagine someone removed it later, washed it and put it back in the kitchen."

Serena tried to understand. The drug was put in the milk to kill Danny. If it had worked and he had been found in the morning, it could have been suggested that he woke in the night in pain and took too many of the pills. There would have been censure, of course, about leaving pills within reach of a child but it would have gone down as a tragic accident.

But that hadn't happened.

Had it?

Serena pressed her hands against her cheeks. She didn't understand. Nothing made sense. The milk must have been drugged because Mr. Richard died and that was the only way he could have been exposed to the drug.

But what happened to Danny? Did he drink some of the milk and was that why he made no outcry when someone took him away in the middle of the night? But why was the glass of milk taken? Surely the missing glass would be noticed. But it didn't matter either way because Danny hadn't been found dead of an overdose.

"Sheriff . . ." Serena had trouble putting it in words. "Sheriff, do you think . . . do you suppose Danny . . ."

"I just don't know, Serena," he said heavily. "But the longer we look and don't find him, the more likely it is that he's dead."

Serena turned away from him and crossed to stare out the window toward the range of mountains. Although it wasn't yet five o'clock, it was almost as dark as dusk and the darkening sky looked close enough to touch, the purplish black clouds blotting out the low hanging sun.

"I've called in the searchers," the sheriff said quietly.

She wanted to protest, to cry out that Danny was so small and the coming storm so huge and violent. Such a storm would terrify grown men caught out in it. What would it do to a little boy? But she knew the sheriff was responsible for the safety of the searchers and they would not be safe in the mountains or on the range tonight.

Sheet lightning exploded in the northwest sky, hanging like a shimmering curtain of fire with the backdrop of immense black thunderclouds.

"It's going to be bad, isn't it?" she asked hopelessly.

"Yes. It's going to be very bad."

"I'll tell Millie to get dinner for the men."

"Most of them will be wanting to load up their horses and get home."

The sheriff was right. Serena waited at the main corral to greet all the men as they came in, to thank them for their help. All of them nodded and said they would come back tomorrow to search again.

"Sure sorry, Serena."

"We looked everywhere. Everywhere."

"Not a trace, Serena. I don't think he's out there."

None of them said what most of them thought, that a body could lie for years undiscovered. They had been looking for a living boy. They hadn't found him. They didn't think anyone would. It was a subdued group of weary men who unsaddled their horses and loaded them into trailers. The pick-ups began to swing out the main ranch road, their headlights already on to pierce the gathering gloom.

Serena stood beside the road watching until the last pick-up was gone. She needed to get up to the house. The sheriff was waiting in the den. He wanted to talk to all of them.

"Hi, Serena."

She turned towards the group of Castle Rock men coming out of the tack room. She nodded to the two professors and realized in surprise that even Howard Minter had apparently joined in the search.

"It's good of all of you to help us," she said as they came up to her.

"That's rugged country," Howard Minter said wearily.

The two professors stopped. "I'm sorry we didn't find him," John Morris said quietly. He looked back toward the mountains. Thunder rumbled ominously and a moment later lightning split the sky. "I hope he has shelter." He reached out, patted Serena's arm. "We'll help look tomorrow."

"Yes, we will," VanZandt agreed quickly.

"Thank you."

They walked on and Serena waited for Peter and Jed. They were the last. And then Serena knew what had nagged her as she watched the searchers ride in to the corral.

"Jed," she called out sharply, "where's Joe?"

Jed and Peter stopped beside her. Both looked exhausted, their shirts stained with sweat and dust.

"Why, I don't know," Jed said slowly. "I thought . . . Hasn't he been here at the stables, helping direct the search?"

"No." She barely squeezed the word from a throat suddenly taut with fear. "No, I haven't seen him all day."

"Well, he has to be around somewhere," Peter said brusquely. "Don't be a fool, Serena."

But the sheriff didn't think Serena was a fool.

Once again men clumped up and down the stairs of the

hacienda. Flashlights flickered across the grounds.

It was clear enough within a half-hour. Joe Walkingstick wasn't to be found.

Millie sat in the kitchen, her apron clutched tightly in her hands, sick fear in her eyes. She told her story over and over, ". . . and when he came down from Danny's room, he brought the dead cat and he told me to be sure and tell Serena. He said he would explain everything to her when she got back from Santa Fe."

Serena had arrived back from Santa Fe at mid-morning. Joe knew how long the drive took. He knew too that she would come immediately when called. So he could have estimated when she would have arrived at the ranch.

He had planned to talk to her then but Serena hadn't seen him.

"Has anyone seen Joe Walkingstick since breakfast?" the sheriff demanded. He looked around the room. One by one, every person shook his head.

The sheriff's face hardened. "All right, folks, let's get one thing straight. I know one of you is lying." He looked at each person in turn. "If any one of you knows anything, now is the time to tell me."

"I object to your tone, Sheriff," Peter said insolently. He lounged against the mantel. Serena looked at him indifferently. It was odd, really. He was as handsome as ever with his vivid blue eyes and wheat blond hair, but she didn't care at all. But she kept her eyes on him. She didn't look at the other corner where Jed stood, his shoulders hunched, his face grim. She couldn't bear to look at Jed.

The sheriff snapped, "What kind of tone would you like, Carey?"

No mister to it. Peter flushed. He wasn't accustomed to being treated brusquely by those he considered his inferiors.

165

"Look, Sheriff, we've spent the whole day looking for Danny. And now because we haven't had any success in the search you've directed, you're trying to blame us. Surely we can't be faulted when a criminal breaks into our home and abducts a child? What progress have you made? Have you checked on reports of escaped criminals? Have you checked on tramps? Just what the hell have you done, Sheriff? Not very damned much, I'd say. And we here at Castle Rock certainly aren't going to tolerate innuendos on the part of incompetent investigators."

Peter's tone was so proprietary. He was so much the duke of the manor speaking to an underling. Serena drew her breath in sharply. Dear God, Peter already saw himself as the owner of Castle Rock.

"The sheriff has done an excellent job," she said forcefully.

Peter turned toward her, arched an eyebrow. "Has he? Then where's Danny?"

"We'll find him," the sheriff said grimly. "And Joe Walkingstick. Alive or dead. And I'll make myself clear to you, Carey, I'm not fooled at all. Not by anyone here. And I'm not afraid of any of you. I don't care how big and powerful you are. Nobody broke in and took that boy. It was an inside job. I'd stake my reputation on it."

"If you make that claim, you just may have to do that, Sheriff," Peter answered angrily. "Now, I'll tell you what I'm going to do. My wife and I are decided on it. We are going to call in the finest private investigator in the state. We'll get to the bottom of this."

"That's not necessary," Serena said loudly. "The sheriff is doing all that anyone can."

Peter lifted his chin and Serena wondered why she had never before realized what an arrogant look he had. "You may not be making the decisions here, Serena."

"What do you mean, Peter?"

"You aren't an heir."

"Why don't you say it straight out, Peter?" she asked angrily.

"Say what?"

"That you think Danny is dead. And if he's dead, you can kick me off the ranch and run it yourself."

A very slight smile touched Peter's face. She would have liked to scratch it, dig her nails deep into his cheeks.

"You've put it well enough, Serena," he said coolly. "And it's time we all faced facts."

"No," she said huskily. "Danny isn't dead. He isn't, do you hear me?"

Thunder crashed like falling steel drums.

Peter turned and looked out the window. "Do you think he's out in that somewhere? If he's on the ranch, why didn't he call out when one of the search parties passed by?"

Serena too looked toward the window and the ghostly radiance of lightning. There wasn't any answer to make. If Danny were alive, he would have shouted for help.

"I'll tell you, Sheriff," Peter continued brusquely, "it's time some real thought was given to this."

For the first time, a tinge of red touched the sheriff's face.

"For instance," Peter demanded, "how does Joe Walkingstick figure in all this?"

"I guess I don't know," the sheriff drawled. "Maybe you can explain it to me."

"Maybe I can. Maybe the answers are pretty simple after all."

"What are you saying, Carey?" Jed asked bluntly.

Peter's eyes narrowed and she knew he didn't like being addressed by his last name by one of the help.

"Yeah, what do you mean, Peter?" Will asked.

Peter ignored Jed and turned to Will. "Look at it. We have a missing kid and a missing Indian. Who knows, maybe Joe had a seizure somewhere or something, but maybe he likes little boys . . ."

The room erupted as Millie flew straight for Peter, her voice high and eerie like an eagle's cry. Peter stumbled back, bloody furrows marking his cheeks. Serena exulted in the attack even as she jumped up to gather Millie in her arms.

"Don't, Millie, he isn't worth it. We know that's a lie. We'd never believe that kind of thing about Joe, never in a million years."

Behind them voices rose, Peter swearing, Julie crying out. Serena ignored the uproar and tried to soothe the furious old woman as she pulled her from the room.

"Just ignore him, Millie. He's a gringo."

"My Joe." Tears slipped down her wrinkled face. "They have hurt my Joe."

Serena kept her arm around Millie's shoulders as they walked down the hall. "Don't be frightened, Millie," she said reassuring. "Maybe Joe had some better idea where Danny might be. Maybe he's still looking."

But Millie was shaking her head. "He was coming back to talk to you and he never came. Now he will never come."

The pain in her voice tore at Serena's heart, and she felt a dreadful sense of foreboding.

They were walking into the kitchen when Jed came up behind them. "Millie," he said abruptly, "I want you to stay in my room tonight. It has a good lock on the door."

Serena looked at him, fear in her eyes. "But why should Millie be in danger?"

"Somebody may not believe she didn't know everything Joe knew."

168

Everything Joe knew. The past tense. Serena swallowed hard. "All right. Millie, perhaps you'd better."

"And you lock your door tonight," Jed ordered Serena.

"I will. You don't have to worry about that." Then she asked sharply, "What are you going to do tonight?"

"I don't know. I'll be here and there."

"Do you think you carry a magic circle with you?"

"What do you mean by that?"

"Why should you be safe if the rest of us aren't?"

His mouth twisted. "I'm going to be damn careful, lady, that's why."

He left then, taking Millie with him.

Serena stood in the kitchen, looked around then wearily started work on dinner.

Julie burst through the door. "Where is that old witch?"

Serena turned around from the stove. "As long as I am manager of this ranch, and I will be until a court order says differently, then Millie is cook here and no one is to give her any trouble."

Julie's lovely face quivered. "Oh Serena, don't be mad at me. I can't help what Peter does—and sometimes I don't like him very much." Tears trembled in her violet eyes.

Serena felt a rush of compassion. She started to speak, then knew she had nothing to say. Peter was Julie's husband. That was a fact, hard and unpalatable, and it made all the difference. Finally, she said, "Look Julie, why don't you give me a hand. Millie has gone to her room and I have to get dinner ready."

Jed came back in a few minutes. He didn't say anything but he nodded and Serena knew Millie was safely in his room. She wished they could talk. Maybe he could make some sense of all of it, but Julie had brightened at his entrance and was smiling up at him.

"Oh Jed, you'll carry this heavy old tray, won't you? I don't think I can budge it."

Somehow Serena got dinner ready for those in the big house and prepared hampers for the dudes to take to their cabins. The storm was obviously going to break at any minute and they didn't want to be caught up at the hacienda.

Dinner at the main table came down to Serena, Julie, Jed, Peter and Will.

Peter glared when Jed joined them but he said nothing. As they ate, Jed spoke to Serena.

"The sheriff told me to tell you he's gone back into town. He says they can't do anything else here tonight. He left a deputy to stay the night."

"Who said he could do that?" Peter demanded.

"I did," Jed answered shortly.

"That's good," Serena said approvingly.

Peter started to speak then frowned and began to eat, his face sullen.

Will toyed with his food. "Joe must be dead," he blurted out.

Everyone looked at him uneasily.

His eyes looked wild. His red hair was rumpled, his face unshaven. "That's right," he said loudly. "Somebody's killed Joe."

"Oh Will, you are such a fool," his sister cried. "Why would anyone kill Joe?"

"Because he knew what happened to Danny. That's right," and he rushed ahead, drowning out her response, "I've been thinking about it. Nobody would bother Joe. That doesn't make any sense. It's all tied up with Danny." Will's face twisted, "I'll tell you, if somebody's hurt Danny and Joe, I'm going to kill the son of a bitch." And he pushed his chair back and stumbled out of the room.

As they looked after him, the lights in the dining room wavered, blinked off, came on again. Sheet lightning seared the sky, streak after brilliant streak. Thunder rolled like a cannonade. Then the storm broke, rain sweeping against the house in sheets.

The wildness of the storm made conversation impossible. They finished eating in silence. Serena and Julie cleared the table and put the dishes in the washer. Neither of them spoke. There wasn't any more to say. No one knew what was happening. Too much had been said, or too little.

As soon as they finished, Serena said good night and started upstairs. The sounds of the storm raged against the house. Outside, the noise would be terrifying.

Could Danny and Joe hear the storm?

Serena ran the final few steps to her room. It seemed another lifetime when she had left it to go to Santa Fe, trying to escape the brooding nemesis at Castle Rock.

But she couldn't escape.

She reached out for her door handle. At least she could bathe and change. Perhaps that would make her feel a little better. She was still wearing the skirt and blouse she had pulled on so quickly that morning in Santa Fe after Will's call came. She felt frowsy and crumpled.

She opened her door and turned on the light. Once again lightning flashed, thunder roared, the lights wavered, then came back on.

Serena stood stone-still in her doorway, staring in shock at her room.

# Fifteen

Someone hated her very much. Very very much. Why else this pointless violence?

The whole long row of Kachinas had been knocked from the shelf into a brilliantly coloured jumble on the floor. And there, just inside the door, lay the remnants of her very favourite, the Ongchoma, ripped and twisted into bits. Serena knelt and began to pick up the pieces of painted cottonwood root, her hands trembling.

Ongchoma was the compassionate Kachina who looks out for children and tries to protect them when they are going to be whipped, touching them so they will feel no pain. Serena held the coloured bits of wood in her hand. Her favourite Kachina. Who could have known that?

Sick at heart, she lay the pieces on her bedside table, then began to pick up the other dolls. None of these, she realized gratefully, has been vandalized, though the Butterfly Maiden Kachina's feathered headdress was bent and the staff of the Black Ogre Kachina was broken. But these could easily be repaired.

When they were all back in place, Serena walked back to the table to look down at the crumpled remains of her favourite doll.

It was deliberate, of course. How could it be otherwise? There were sixty-four of the Kachinas. It was too much to ask that she believe her very favourite had been destroyed by chance. Entirely too much to ask.

Serena shivered. Who could have known how much that particular doll meant to her?

She held the fragments and remembered the day Joe Walkingstick had given it to her. She had been in the hospital in Santa Fe, thirteen years old and frightened, her throat a fury of pain. She had cried to come home to Castle Rock, certain she would feel better there. She had lain in her bed, her throat a burning agony, and looked up to see Joe in the doorway, holding Ongchoma in his hands. He brought the doll to her and explained how Ongchoma made little children feel better, saved them from pain. When he left, the doll rested in her arm and she felt better and no one could persuade her to let go of it.

Only Joe would know what that doll meant to her. Only Joe . . . Through the years, no matter what happened, a twisted ankle, a broken date, an unkind slight, she had managed to smile at Joe—well, Ongchoma will make it feel better.

Now the little doll was destroyed and couldn't be put together again. Just like her world at Castle Rock.

She sighed. Only Joe knew . . . Then she stood very still, looking at the pale peach spread on her bed. There on the bed . . . Yes, it was a piece of the fox skin ruff Ongchoma wore around his neck.

Why would the Kachina have been on her bed?

If Joe wanted to leave a message for her, what better place to secrete it than in the doll he knew to be her favourite? If she had come to her room this morning when she arrived from Santa Fe and seen the doll on her bed, she would have known it meant something and she would have looked until she found the message.

But she hadn't come upstairs at all.

Who had come to her room?

And what could Joe's message have been? Why hadn't he come back from where he was on the ranch and talked to her?

Could it be that he was afraid to come. That he didn't want to see a particular person?

So he left her a message.

Hours ago.

Serena looked toward the rain-flooded window. The storm assailed the foot-thick adobe walls. The wind howled, a high eerie keening like witches wailing.

Hours ago someone slipped into her room, saw the Kachina, guessed at its purpose. Hours ago. The message read, the intruder ripped the Kachina apart, then pulled down the rest of the dolls to hide what had happened.

Now she was left with broken bits of a doll and no hope of learning the message it had held.

Serena's fingers tightened onto the pieces of painted root. What could Joe have wanted to tell her? And where would he have told her to come to meet with him privately?

Think, she told herself angrily.

She had gone to Santa Fe, asked Joe to keep watch over Danny. Joe was absolutely dependable. She would bet her life on Joe. That was why, really, Will's phone call reporting Danny missing had been so shocking. Although no one could have expected Joe to foresee a kidnapping . . .

Serena stood very still, scarcely breathing.

What was it Joe had told Millie? He told her that Danny would be all right, that the Kachinas would care for Danny. Joe was sure of Danny's safety.

Oh my God, Serena thought, of course, it made every kind of sense. Why hadn't she seen it before? She should have known. Joe always did his job.

Joe must have come up to Danny's room last night to

check on him and found the dead cat. Or perhaps Mr. Richard wasn't dead yet, perhaps he was sleeping heavily, his breath drawn thickly through an open mouth, obviously drugged. It wouldn't take Joe long to spot the milk and the almost empty capsule of pills and to realize that Danny was in deadly danger.

A sleeping boy. A dead cat. A dark house. And somewhere near, a killer who stepped quietly in the night. Joe's first responsibility was to protect Danny. What would happen if he raised an alarm? He didn't have the authority to call the police. That would have to be done by Will or Julie or Peter.

Obviously, Joe hadn't believed he could prevail so he must have taken Danny somewhere to hide him, then intended to meet her on her return the next morning and tell her what had happened.

But she hadn't come to her room, hadn't found the message.

When had the Kachina been destroyed? How long ago? Oh God, how long ago?

Serena whirled around, hurried to her closet. She changed into Levis, a flannel shirt, boots and her poncho. She was dropping it over her head when she heard a low knock on her door.

Quickly, she turned off the light then stepped back into an alcove. She had no time to talk to anyone.

The door handle turned, the door edged open.

"Serena?"

Her heart ached. She loved the sound of his voice.

"Serena." He spoke louder.

She stood frozen in the dark. Could she trust him? She knew the answer. No. He was too mysterious, his appearance on the ranch too fortuitous. And how could she trust a man who would look at her as he did then make love to Julie.

"Damn," he said angrily and the door slammed shut.

Serena waited a long five minutes. She couldn't afford to run into Jed. Still, she felt a frantic impulse to hurry.

When she opened her door to dark and quiet, she slipped down the stairs, listening as she went. First she would find the deputy. He could get in touch with the Sheriff. She had an idea where Joe might be waiting for her. Castle Rock wasn't the only place on the ranch with caves. She and Will and Julie had played in a favourite cave for years. It was in a sandstone cliff just beneath the biggest cottonwood tree on the ranch.

Serena paused at the foot of the steps. The hacienda lay quiet as a tomb. She shivered. Everyone had withdrawn this stormy night. She walked quietly down the hall. The only light came through the windows from the huge uneven flashes of sheet lightning.

She looked in all the downstairs rooms but found no one. Then she saw a crack of light beneath the kitchen door. She felt a rush of relief. The deputy must be having a snack. She pushed through the swinging door and started to call out, but the kitchen was empty.

Serena paused in the doorway. Someone must be about but she didn't want to call out. The bright empty room frightened her. Where could the deputy be?

Well, she didn't have time for this. Quickly, she crossed to the telephone. She would call the sheriff. She picked up the receiver and there was no sound at all on the line.

It could be the storm, of course. This kind of storm often whipped the lines until they broke. Sometimes they lost service for several days. Of course, it could be the storm.

But where was the deputy and why did the hacienda have this awful waiting silence about it?

Serena quickly replaced the receiver then looked fearfully

around the bright kitchen. There was something so terrifying in the absolute stillness.

The deputy gone. The phone dead. The dark rooms beyond the brightly-lit kitchen.

Serena fled from the kitchen. She hesitated in the dark foyer. She felt so alone and frightened.

Will.

She could trust Will. If there was no one else in the world left for her to trust, she could trust him. With a tremendous sense of relief, she ran back up the stairs and down the dark hallway to his room. She turned the knob, stepped inside, again into darkness.

"Will," she whispered, "Will, I need . . ."

She turned on the light. The bed lay untouched. Serena looked frantically around, but Will wasn't there.

Through the uncurtained windows, lightning crackled. Rain flooded against the glass panes.

She didn't like summer storms. They frightened her. She had always been careful to be safe at home when they struck. But tonight the hacienda held more terror than the storm.

Serena turned off the light and left Will's empty room behind, leaving, too, part of her certainty in what she could trust to be good and right. She crept down the stairs, feeling now that only danger could be abroad in the dark rooms. She reached the den and threaded her way around dark clumps of furniture to the gun case. Reaching up on the ledge, she found the key and opened the case. She carefully lifted out the Winchester rifle from the second slot. Using the same key, she unlocked the drawer beneath the cabinet and felt until she found the right cartridge boxes. She slipped two of them deep into the pocket of her poncho after loading the rifle.

She knew guns, knew bullets. Thanks to Uncle Dan she

could shoot very well indeed. She could drop a running coyote at fifty yards.

Perhaps that would come as a surprise to someone tonight.

The house still seemed deserted when she reached the front door. She edged it open, then slipped out onto the porch. The house lay dark and quiet as the hulk of a drowned boat. She could feel menace, sense it in the brooding lifelessness of the house behind her. She plunged out into the battering rain almost with a sense of relief.

A gigantic spear of lightning exploded above her, splitting into jagged prongs that lit the night with a ghostly radiance. The rain came down so thick that it shimmered like a curtain of silver.

The rain struck Serena with physical force, pelting her head and shoulders. She pulled the hood of the poncho low over her face and ran from memory, her boots slipping in the inches-deep water.

Serena was breathless by the time she reached the door of the stables. She had never ridden Hurricane in this kind of weather. He was a steady, serious horse. Would he panic and bolt when the big lightning flashes danced above him? But there was no other way to reach the cave.

The cave might lie empty, might be a musty bat-stop on the way to nowhere.

But Joe had to be somewhere.

She opened the stable door and started to step inside. Light spilled out of the tack room. Boots gritted against concrete.

Serena dodged to her left and crouched at the end of the stalls.

A stall door opened and a horse moved uneasily. A man swore and grunted as he slapped the saddle atop the horse and cinched it. Then footsteps came toward the end of the stables.

Serena saw them pass. She saw his face, strained and hard, a frightening distortion of a face she knew so well. As the stable door slammed shut behind horse and rider, Serena was torn by relief and sadness.

It wasn't Jed. Oh God, it wasn't Jed! But pain twisted inside her. She had grown up with Will. She had been sure in her heart that she could always count on Will.

She tried to shut the memory of his misery-ridden face from her mind as she saddled Hurricane. It did no good to think. She must not think, she must only move and do this night. She would not think.

She slid the rifle into its long holster and led Hurricane to the door. When she opened it and the rain's spume slanted inside, Hurricane stiffened his legs. She patted his shoulder and talked softly to him. Then she mounted and gently urged him forward. Hurricane hesitated for just an instant then he moved.

The rain splashed over them like the thundering wash from a waterfall. Hurricane stepped jerkily for a few minutes, then, as if to say, well, all right, whatever you want, he settled into a steady trot.

They couldn't see, of course. The night was a wild melange of darkness and brief wavering light, slatting water and rushing rivulets, but they kept going, trusting to memory, to their years together, to a knowledge born of experience.

Serena strained to see whenever the lightning burned the night sky, but she found no trace of Will.

Should she have hurried faster, tried to follow him? But she had to trust her own hunch. She had to find Joe.

Usually, it took ten minutes to ride the broad flat trail that ended on a bluff overlooking the river. Tonight, she struggled through the wind and rain for almost a half-hour. Her hands were numb with cold by the time she reined in Hurricane beneath the cottonwood tree that bent and creaked in the wind. She dismounted, dropping the reins in front of Hurricane.

The storm's fury struck her full force when she began her descent. The wind howled and shrieked around her. Rain pummeled her back. Serena edged carefully down, clinging to exposed roots and sharp edged bits of rock.

She almost missed the cave mouth. It was even narrower than she remembered, an oblique slit in the rock face, half-hidden by a boulder.

Serena paused in the narrow opening. Darkness pressed against her eyes.

"Joe?"

She whispered and the light sound of her voice vanished into emptiness.

"Joe."

She yanked the flashlight out of her pocket and switched it on. Dark shapes began to move above her, fluttering and turning, a band of bats startled into motion.

The flashlight beam dipped toward the back of the cave then froze like a stage spotlight until it began to bounce, throwing wild shadows against the walls, as Serena half-ran, half-stumbled the length of the cave to drop beside a still figure.

# Sixteen

Serena's hands trembled uncontrollably. The light wavered up and down but she could see clearly, too clearly. The back of Joe's head looked soft and misshapen and dark brownish splotches of blood spread thickly beside him.

She reached out, touched the hand curled so defence-lessly. Cold. Cold and stiff.

Serena huddled beside him, her head pressed against her knees. She didn't cry. There would be time later for tears. She sat in an agony of loss and horror.

If she hadn't gone in to Santa Fe . . . Oh Joe, Joe . . .

Finally, she lifted her head and stared sombrely at his body. It was so clear now what had happened. Joe had taken Danny away from the hacienda, hidden him to keep him safe, then he left a message for Serena in the Kachina doll. But someone else found and read that message and came to the cave.

Serena stared at the bloodied back of Joe's head. That told a story, too. The killer must have claimed Serena sent him, must have gained Joe's confidence.

Serena worked it out. The killer came to the cave, talked to Joe, pretended Serena had sent him. Joe, glad perhaps to share the responsibility of Danny, must have revealed the boy's hiding-place. Then they turned to go, Joe leading the way, and, savagely, brutally, a raised hand slammed down-ward.

181

Stiffly, Serena started to get up. The flashlight dipped forward. Abruptly, Serena held it steady, focussed the beam just beyond Joe's outstretched hand.

Blood dries a dark brown.

Joe had almost finished his message. Thin uneven letters straggled away into a smear. But there was enough. ANASA and part of a Z. Joe had used his last weakening spurt of life to try and save Danny.

How much time, Serena wondered, did she have? Or had time already run out for Danny? Had someone stalked him as he waited for Joe to return to the cliff-side dwellings built so long ago by the Anasazi, the Old People. The golden adobe ruins clung to the cliff, accessible only by a man-made footbridge or by a narrow rock bridge that curved over the canyon.

Time or no time, Serena had no choice. She must go. She was Danny's only chance, slim as it might be. If she returned to the ranch, the killer would have plenty of time to find Danny and kill him—making it possible to rid the ranch of Serena, making it safe to use the ranch for every kind of smuggling.

When she came out of the cave, the storm took her breath away, the rain water blinded her. Another time she would have thought the climb back up the bluff impossible, but tonight the desperate frantic determination to reach Danny propelled her up.

Hurricane stood waiting with his back to the sharply slanting rain. Serena mounted and turned his head toward the mountain path. He held back for just a moment, then, when she insisted, started forward.

Wonderful horse. Gallant, courageous, superb horse. Soon they were flying through the darkness, both of them straining ahead, the rain and thunder and jagged streaks of lightning surrounding them like a devil's chorus. As they climbed higher, moved up into the fir-thick forest, the trees absorbed the violence of the rain but the lightning danced and crackled in the tree tops. Off to the left, a tree blazed. Serena's yellow poncho glistened in the smoky light.

She made the turn that led up to the cliff houses and knew the hardest part lay ahead. She didn't dare use the rope bridge. She would be too vulnerable, too open to attack.

That left the rock bridge.

Once she paused, thinking she heard movement behind her but strain as she might she couldn't distinguish any sound from the creaking of the trees and the moaning of the wind and the almost incessant roll of thunder, deep and heavy as wagon wheels crossing a wooden bridge.

She slowed Hurricane to a cautious walk as they neared the canyon. Abruptly, Hurricane stopped and Serena knew they must be near the precipitous cliff edge. She dismounted and risked a quick look with the flash. Yes, there was the edge only feet away. She turned the light off and welcomed the night's embrace. A killer moved somewhere near her. Light could betray her.

It was obvious, of course, why the killer had to wait until tonight to go after Danny. He had managed to break away from his search group this morning to find Joe, but there hadn't been time to go after Danny. Besides, one of the search parties might see him and he couldn't afford to be glimpsed near the cliff dwellings. The search parties must have checked there today but Joe would have told Danny to keep very quiet and there wouldn't be time to look in all the hundreds of rooms.

Once the killer murdered Joe, he had felt secure in the knowledge that only he knew Danny's hiding place. He could wait for the cover of night to slip up the mountain to the cliff dwellings.

He hadn't counted on the ferocity of the storm.

Or on Serena.

So there still should be time. If she could reach the canyon before him or soon after . . .

Serena hesitated at the cliff's edge. Far below water roared as it churned through the narrow canyon, bubbling and swirling, a roiling implacable mass. She must decide what to do about Hurricane. He couldn't make the descent, not in the rain and dark, though the intensity of the storm was beginning to lessen. If she hung the reins down in front, he would wait until she returned. But she needed desperately to get word to Castle Rock. Reaching up, she rubbed Hurricane gently behind an ear.

Could he possibly understand what she wanted him to do?

It was worth a try.

It meant turning the light back on, keeping it on interminably long seconds. When she finished, she looked at it and wondered if anyone would ever see it.

It depended upon how closely they looked at her saddle. But a riderless horse occasions a close look. That had to be her hope. She stared down at the saddle, at the word, Anasazi, scratched across the leather. The metal tip on the end of her reins had gouged out the letters which straggled unevenly against the dark wet leather.

ANASAZI.

All right. She slipped the rifle out of the holster, patted Hurricane one more time, then lifted the reins, tied them in a loose knot over the saddle horn, turned him to head down the trail and slapped him gently on the rump. "Go home, Hurricane, go home."

The horse moved a step or two away then looked back over his shoulder. She slapped his rump again. "Home, Hurricane, home."

He began to move away and then he was gone.

Serena turned, covered the flashlight so only the merest gleam showed, and started down the steep slippery trail. The lower she went, the louder the roaring water sounded beneath her. She knew it would be a terrifying spectacle to see, the foaming mass of water bounding between the narrow canyon walls, carrying boulders and tree trunks.

Soon she must cross above that violently rushing water.

It was sooner and worse than she expected.

The natural bridge spanned the fifteen-foot wide chasm. Serena could remember clambering over it, like a monkey in a ship's rigging, when she was little and they came to the cliff dwelling for picnics. But those were sunny days and the rock was dry.

She risked a full sweep of light over the bridge then wished she hadn't. It glimmered mistily, the stone glistening with wetness. The rain fell now in a gentle sweep, making the rock glassy and dangerous to hold, slick as mica.

She didn't point the light down into the canyon. She didn't want to see the foaming hurtling water.

She stuffed the flash back into her poncho pocket and stood thoughtfully, holding the rifle.

She needed both hands to cross.

But a merciless killer was somewhere near, perhaps waiting on the other side, perhaps coming up hard behind, hurrying to remove the obstacle to his domination of Castle Rock.

Serena reached inside the slicker, undid her belt and pulled it off. She threaded it through the trigger guard of the rifle, closed the belt and slipped it over her head and the rifle hung down her back.

Edging out onto the rock, she felt her boots start to slip at her first step. Dropping to her knees, she reached out with her hands and carefully began to inch out, moving ever so slowly up to the highest point of the arch then starting down the other side.

Beneath her the water swept by with the roar of an avalanche.

She was within reach of the other side when the ridge of rock she clung to began to move.

There was no time to scream, no time to pray, no time to envision the horror that awaited her, the strangling maelstrom of water that would bludgeon her against the canyon walls.

Her fingers dug into the slippery rock face but she was sliding and then she plunged over the side. The fall tilted her backwards. Before she could scream, she felt as if her chest were caught in a vice and then she realized that, incredibly, she wasn't falling any longer.

Serena dangled over the roaring water. It took her a long moment to understand that an up-thrust limb from a dead tree had speared through the loop the belt made and caught her as neatly as a horseshoe locking onto a post. She reached out, grabbed the tree limb and clung. When she stopped trembling, she carefully undid the belt, caught the rifle, and awkwardly began to climb up the canyon wall, pulling from one bush up to the next, until she clambered safely over onto the ledge beside the rock bridge.

She lay there for a long moment, gathering strength, then rose and began to move along the narrow ribbon of rock that led around a bluff to the cliff dwellings.

She knew the way. She had been here so many times as a little girl with Julie and Will and Uncle Dan, scampering along the tops of the houses. The cream colour of the adobe houses merged into the dusty golden-red of the cliff. The overhang protected the houses from above and the sheer drop beneath protected them from the canyon floor. On a summer morning with the cicadas singing, the cliff houses hung between sky and ground, a child's dream of sanctuary.

Serena walked very quietly. The only sound came from the throaty roar of the water in the canyon below. The rain swirled in a gentle mist now. The storm was over and soon the high waters would recede as quickly as they had come. Now only a gentle drip from the houses made a light sound. Beyond that, silence stretched as thick and heavy as the black night sky.

She stepped slowly around the curve of the cliff. The houses began just past here. It was utterly quiet, utterly dark, not a sign of life anywhere.

Then Serena drew her breath in sharply. That gritty scraping sound. Someone moved quietly, oh so quietly, along the second tier of houses.

Then the voice sounded above her and Serena's skin prickled.

"Danny? It's hard to find my way in the dark. Where are you?"

It sounded just like Joe Walkingstick, a tenor sing song with a drawl.

But Joe was dead. Joe lay stiffly in a cave down near the river, the back of his head misshapen and bloody.

"Danny, it's me, Joe."

"Danny!" Serena shouted. Her voice rang clearly between the canyon walls. "Danny, don't answer. It isn't Joe. Joe's dead."

Danny's clear thin voice sounded just feet from her. "Serena, where are you?"

"Danny, be quiet, be quiet!"

Serena began to run. If she could reach Danny first, well, they could hold off an army. Please God, she willed, don't let him call out again.

The only sound came from the scuff of her boot heels as she ran carefully along the top of the second tier of houses. When she judged she must be close to Danny, she stopped and whistled softly, making a silvery liquid sound like the faraway call of an owl. From almost beneath her feet she heard her answer whoo-oo, whoo-oo. She took a few more steps then knelt and patted the adobe roof until she found the opening. "Danny, are you here?"

"Yes. Oh, Serena, what did you mean? What's happened to Joe? Where . . ."

"Shh. I'll tell you . . ."

The light came directly at her, shocking her into immobility, blinding her for an instant.

He kicked the rifle out of her hands. Serena tried to lunge after it.

"Hold still, Serena. Or I'll shoot Danny."

He spoke in his own voice now. He said it almost casually, as if it didn't matter very much.

Serena crouched unmoving. Then slowly, she turned to face the bright beam of light and the dark shadow that stood behind it.

"Hello, Peter." She spoke quietly, as if they stood in the den, talking of weather or cattle or fencing. Slowly, she stood upright. She cradled her right wrist in her left hand. It hurt terribly from Peter's kick. But that didn't matter. "I should have known it was you."

"Oh, I don't know," he said pleasantly, "I was rather clever about it all."

"You are the smuggler."

"Of course, my dear. Who else would have the wit to plan it all?"

Oh Jed, she thought heartbrokenly, I thought it was you. Jed, I'm so sorry and now I will never have the chance to tell you how much I care, how wrong I was . . .

"You've almost ruined the most important delivery of all, Serena. I can't have that."

"I don't suppose you can."

Did she see something moving in the darkness behind him? Was there a blacker shadow there or was she only hoping? If she could keep him talking.

"The most important delivery?"

"Right. Eighteen million dollars' worth of cocaine, Serena. Think of it. Eighteen million dollars." His voice caressed the words. "Eighteen million dollars. I can buy the world."

Cocaine. Bloody snow. The innocent looking white crystalline powder that comes into the United States on the blood of innocent people, creating a traffic that destroys anything in its path.

"So that's why you killed Uncle Dan."

"So you've figured that out, too?" His voice was harder now. "You know something, Serena, you're too smart for your own good. Way too smart."

"You tried to stop me, too," she said quickly, hoping to hide behind her voice the tell-tale sounds of movement behind him. "You put the rattler in Hurricane's stall."

"It would have made a nice accident but . . ." He lunged toward Serena and abruptly she was in front of him, held hard by one arm. A cold hard circle of metal pressed behind her right ear.

"Don't move, Shelton, or I'll blow her head off."

The arm that pinioned her still held the flashlight. It pointed now where he had stood, limning Jed in the bright circle of light.

"Quite a party we're having here," Peter said a little breathlessly. "So you're a narc, Shelton. I thought you were. But you came after the wrong man tonight."

"Let go of her, Carey. You're surrounded."

"Oh?" Peter's voice was amused. "Somehow, Shelton, I don't believe you."

The lights came on then, a half dozen of them, all locked on her and Peter.

She looked up. His face was oddly expressionless and somehow that was even more frightening.

"Let go of her," Jed shouted.

"Sorry, old man. She's coming with me. All the way."

Peter began to move her ahead of him toward the edge of the cliff. When they stood at the very rim, Peter called out, "I must have free passage. If not, I'll throw her in." He paused and they all could hear the rumble of the surging water. "And don't think you can shoot me first. We're right on the edge and she'll go over."

"You can't get away with it." The sheriff's deep voice echoed against the canyon walls. "We'll get you."

"But if you do," and Peter's voice was light and pleasant and unruffled, "why then Serena will be very, very dead."

Serena could feel the thudding of his heart, the tension in his body.

Suddenly Jed yelled, "Oh no, oh God no!"

It was like being caught up in a riptide, flung out of control, powerless. She and Peter were slammed back from the edge, then they were thrashing in a melee. She heard a low ferocious growl and realized that Will had wrapped his huge arms around both of them and thrown them heavily back from the edge.

Peter's grip on her abruptly slackened. She rolled free from the flailing arms and legs and suddenly, blessedly, Jed was there, holding her and saying over and over, "Oh Serena, Serena, Serena."

"Watch out!"

The shout sounded at the same time as the pistol shot.

Serena struggled to see from out of Jed's protecting arms.

The lights still pinioned Will and Peter against the red ground. Will's huge arm crooked around Peter's neck, tighter and tighter, but Peter still held the gun and blood welled from Will's side. Still, Will held on, tighter and tighter, drawing Peter's head back and back and back. Then it was over, Peter's hand lolling lifelessly against Will and the hand with the gun falling limply to the ground.

Serena struggled away from Jed and ran to fall beside them, pulling and tugging to move Peter's body and reaching out with her hand to try to stop the rush of blood from Will's side.

# Seventeen

Serena came out of the intensive care unit. The first streaks of dawn sifted into the silent corridor from a high narrow window. She sighed wearily and looked dully at the floor.

"Serena."

Her head jerked up. Somehow she had never expected Jed to come here. He must have come about Will. Do you arrest a man struggling for his life?

She blurted out her first thought. "Will saved my life."

Jed came slowly toward her. A stubble of beard covered his cheeks. His eyes looked hollow and weary.

"Yes, Serena. I know he did. Is he . . . Have they said . . ."

"Whether he will live? They think so. But Jed, he'd rather die than be shut away. It would . . ."

"Don't worry, Serena," he said quickly. "It's going to be all right."

"But Will was . . ." She stopped, unwilling to say it.

"Will was one of them. I know."

"That's why you came to Castle Rock." It wasn't a question. It was a statement.

"That's why I came."

"You're a . . . what did Peter call you? A narc?"

"I guess you can put it like that. Actually, I really am a cowboy. It's my brother who was an agent for the Drug Enforcement Agency." Jed's face looked grim. "He was the one who first figured Peter as head of a big ring." Jed rubbed his

192

cheek. "Paul was gunned down in Miami five months ago. The agency let me take his place. I swore I'd get Carey." He sighed wearily. "And now I have. He'll never smuggle another ounce of cocaine. Do you know how much he brought into the U.S. this year, Serena?"

She shook her head.

"Eight hundred and forty-six pounds. But that doesn't tell the half of it. It doesn't tell you about the lives that are ruined, the murders, the bribery, the crawling rottenness that infects everyone who touches cocaine smuggling."

"I know." And in a way she did. Uncle Dan dead. Will hurt and in terrible trouble. And Julie . . .

"He was a nasty bastard," Jed continued, his voice hard. "A nasty bastard. He came to Castle Rock last year, looking for a good landing place, and he liked what he saw so he gave Julie a big rush . . ."

Yes, Serena thought, after he figured out I had no real claim to Castle Rock. That's when he turned to Julie.

"Poor little Julie," Jed said quietly.

Serena heard the pity and kindness in his voice and her heart ached. So he really did care for Julie. She had been right to run away to Santa Fe. It was Julie he really loved. Serena looked away. All right. Julie needed him. She really did. And now Castle Rock would be safe for Danny so she could leave.

The corridor looked blanched in the early morning light, pale and ghostly and gray. A gray, gray world, but that's the kind of world it was.

"Do you know what Julie told me?" Jed continued.

"No. No. What did she say?"

"She said it had been such hell, that she was so afraid of him these last few months. It was because of her that Will cooperated, of course. Peter told Will that Julie was in it up to her neck, that if he went to jail, she would go, too. That was the club he held over Will. And he told him the planes were just bringing marijuana. They were bringing it, too, but the big money came from the cocaine."

Serena's throat was suddenly dry. "Oh Jed, what will they do to Will?"

Jed looked almost as if he might reach out to touch her but he didn't. "Will's going to be all right. He's already cooperated with us. Without him we couldn't have arrested the Minters and . . ."

"The Minters!"

"Oh yes, they were part of the distribution ring, funneling the stuff to the West Coast."

"The Minters. I should have known. But I thought it was the professors and . . ."

"And me?"

She didn't look at him. You can't look at a man when you have admitted thinking he was a crook.

"You did come out of the blue, and you searched Will's room and you told me you finished at Texas, and they didn't have any record of it."

Jed smiled tiredly. "Well, I don't blame you. But I wasn't using my full name. I did graduate, but as Jed Shelton Royce."

Jed Royce. It had a nice sound. Jed Royce. But it didn't matter now how his name sounded.

"And the professors?" she continued quickly. "Why were they always out on horseback? And why were their papers locked up in a trunk?"

He answered the last question first. "They really couldn't afford to have you see their papers. They were busy writing up the records of their excavations."

"Excavations?"

"They are archaeologists and they pretended to be

194

working on a physics text so they could be close to the Anasazi ruins. They wanted me to tell you they are really very sorry for the deception."

"Oh, that's all right," she said quickly. She even managed a smile. "I'm glad they weren't mixed up in it. I like them. Both of them." Then her smile slipped away. Really, there was nothing to smile about. Joe dead. Will hurt. Julie a widow. And, Jed . . .

They looked at each other sombrely. He reached out then to touch her lightly on the cheek.

"I'm sorry that we lost control of it, Serena. I finally confided in the sheriff who I was. I'd decided I could trust him."

"Trust him?"

"Yes. You wouldn't know it, but half the time the local law enforcement people have been bought off. DEA agents can't trust anybody."

"Oh."

"But I'd pretty well decided Sheriff Coulter was all right. But neither he nor I tumbled to the fact that Joe had hidden Danny to keep him safe. We both thought Peter had taken him, intending to kill him so that he could gain control of the ranch."

"Instead," Serena said slowly, "Peter found the note in the Kachina. That led him to Joe."

Jed nodded. "He persuaded Joe to tell him where Danny was."

They didn't put the rest of it into words; Joe turning and walking toward the cave entrance, Peter behind him . . .

Jed frowned. "We were watching Peter, of course. But he knocked out the deputy and gave us the slip. Thank God Will was suspicious."

"So Will followed him to the cliff dwellings," Serena said quietly.

"Yes." He smiled at her. "We have to thank you for leading the rest of us there."

"Me?"

"We stopped Hurricane as he was heading back to the stables."

ANASAZI. She and Joe had both done their best.

"Still, it was Will who saved us."

"Yes," Jed agreed. "If it hadn't been for Will you and Danny would have been in bad shape." His face tightened. "Do you know what he was going to do to Danny?"

She shook her head.

"He had this one planned, too. Another accident."

"Another one? But what . . ."

"We found a gunny sack where he had dropped it. It had a gila monster in it."

A rattlesnake for her. A gila monster for Danny. For an instant, Serena pictured a little boy lying there in the dusty dark, unable to get up and run, and the awful moments he would have spent after Peter opened the sack and loosed the lizard. The dreadful, terrifying, panic-filled moments.

A flash of white brought her back to the hospital corridor. A nurse moved past them on rubber-soled heels. She darted a curious glance at them.

We must look a mess, Serena thought absently, muddy and bedraggled and worn. If she could just think of unimportant facts like these and not look ahead . . .

"It's all over now, Serena," Jed was saying, his voice gentle. Almost loving. That's what she would think . . . except for Julie. But it was clear now. It was Julie he cared about. And Julie needed love.

Everyone needs love, Serena thought bleakly, but to some it doesn't come.

"Come on, Serena, don't look so unhappy. It really is all

over but the shouting. Will's given us the information on the next shipment. We'll be waiting for them when the plane lands at Castle Rock. Then it will be all over for the ranch."

"And what will you do, Jed?" Her throat ached so she could scarcely get the words out.

"I don't know," he said slowly. "I had thought once about seeing if I could keep my job at Castle Rock but . . ."

"That would be wonderful," Serena said stiffly. "I know Julie needs you . . ."

"Julie?" he interrupted.

She had started and now she must finish, though the words hurt, every one of them. "Well, I know you are in love with Julie and . . ."

He reached out then, his hands gripping her arms so hard she almost cried out but her heart hurt too much for any other pain to matter.

"Why yes," she said. "I saw you kissing her and," she could feel tears burning behind her eyes, but she mustn't cry, dear God, she mustn't, "that's when I knew you didn't care . . . for . . . me."

Her eyes brimmed over with tears.

"Love Julie?" he repeated, his voice incredulous, "Oh Serena, no. Not Julie. It's you. Serena, I love you."

"But you . . . I saw you and Julie . . ."

He grimaced. "I don't . . . Hell, I felt like such a bastard. But I had to find out more about Peter. It was part of my job. A lousy part."

"Then you never cared for Julie?"

"No. It's you. But that's no good, is it?"

She caught her breath.

"I mean, obviously you love Will. So I guess . . . I guess when it's over, well, it will be goodbye."

"Oh Jed, you fool. You wonderful crazy fool."

He looked up, startled.

"Oh Jed, you idiot. Of course I love Will."

Jed's face sagged.

"I love him like a brother. But I love you . . ." and then there was no more air or space to tell him as he gathered her up in his arms and his mouth closed over hers and the two of them were together and love burst like a flame between them.